CRAZY HEARTS

ANNABETH SARYU

ANNABETH SARYU
Heal. Heart. Happy Endings

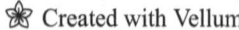 Created with Vellum

PROLOGUE

Mike

Early Spring, Chicago IL

That son of a bitch has done it again.

It's no surprise he can kick my ass. It's not that I suck, it's just Madman Markovski is that good.

No, what really pisses me off is that he's made me look like an ass. In front of Coach and the other guys. In front of Louise.

What the hell does she see in him, anyway?

"Mike Daughtry?" A young, edgy-looking nurse calls my name from the waiting room door.

"Here we go, Mike." Coach Rodgers stands and puts a hand on my arm as I navigate to the door with an ice pack covering my eye.

We stop in front of her, and she looks at us both, then smiles at me. "You must be Mr. Daughtry."

"Yeah." I shift the ice pack away from my eye to see her better.

"And you are?" she turns toward Rodgers.

"I'm his coach," he explains. "I brought him in."

"This way, please."

We follow her past a long narrow sea of desks to a cluster of small rooms.

"Hey, um, do you need me anymore?" Rodgers asks at the doorway. "I'd like to get back to work if that's okay. But if I need to stay, it's not a problem."

"Nope," the nurse answers. "He's a legal adult, and he's conscious. We're good."

"Take off, Coach. If I need anything, I'll call my sister. Or my dad."

"Let's hope it doesn't come to that," Rodgers replies. "Let me know what happens. If you need me to come back, seriously, it's not a problem."

"Sure. Thanks." I wave at him with my free hand.

Rodgers nods at both of us before disappearing out the exit. The nurse bobs her head toward a triage area, and I follow her into a small room.

"Please have a seat on the bed, Mr. Daughtry." The nurse pulls a curtain in front of the door as she speaks. Petite but curvy, she's shorter than me even when I'm sitting down.

She drops onto a small stool facing me and types onto a laptop suspended from a pull-out shelf on the wall.

"What happened to you, Mr. Daughtry?"

"Mr. Daughtry is my dad. Please call me Mike."

"Sure. What happened to you, Mike?"

"Sparring accident. Got punched in the eye."

"Sparring?" Ink-black eyes look up from the computer in surprise. "As in you're some kind of... professional fighter?"

"Yeah. I fight out of DeadFall MMA."

"I see. Were you wearing any protective gear when the injury occurred?"

"Nope."

"That's some accident." She concentrates on the screen as her fingers rap viciously on the keyboard. "How's the other guy? Is he out in the waiting room, too?"

"Nope." I snort in disgust. "Knowing him, he's probably getting off with the woman who caused all this as we speak."

The rapid-fire typing comes to a screeching halt. "The woman who caused all this?" She rolls her eyes. "What'd she do? Drag you both by the hair into a room and tell you to beat the hell out of each other?"

"No." I cross my arms, dropping the ice pack from my face.

"Ah." She studies my face for a few minutes. It must be a mess because she doesn't speak for a long time. "So, you guys acted like Neanderthals, but it's what's-her-name's fault?"

"Neanderthal? Is that a medical term?" I ask.

"Some days," she replies. "We'll just chalk this up to a work-related accident. Sound about right?"

"Yeah."

"Are you taking any medications?"

"No."

The feisty demon resumes typing for a few seconds, then stops. She stands and dons a pair of blue gloves. "I need to take your vitals and have a look at the eye, okay?"

"That's why I'm here."

"Keep the ice on it for now."

I nod and she pops an electronic thermometer under my tongue. Up close, Feisty's kinda cute. She's got this edgy haircut that's shaved around the sides and back, with long black hair growing on top. It's dyed an iridescent blue on the ends and around her face. I rarely like short hair on women, but it calls out her unusual striking features.

It suits her well. Very well.

When the thermometer beeps, Feisty notes the reading and tosses the plastic casing into the trash. But when she tries to fasten a blood pressure cuff around my arm, those delicate hands struggle to wrap it tightly around my well-developed bicep.

"You need to use the extra-large one," I tell her.

She flushes and attempts to smooth the short sleeve of my shirt up to make more room for the cuff at the top. When it doesn't work, she heads over to a set of drawers. She returns and applies the larger cuff to my arm while I study the baby-pink skin under oval fingernails, a delicate contrast to her pearl-white complexion.

When the machine beeps, she returns to the computer and records the data.

"Everything good?" I ask after a silent pause.

"So far," she confirms before snapping on another pair of gloves. "Need to see your eye now."

Feisty comes close and her fingers gently pry my hand away from where I hold the icepack over my eye. As she focuses on the injury, I count the number of tiny colored studs along her earlobe that extend up to a plain silver ear cuff. Pink. Blue, red. Diamond.

"Someone did a good job patching this up." She runs a gentle finger along the steri-strips holding the skin together alongside my eye socket.

"Yeah." I push away images of Louise's skilled hands treating me.

"The doctor should be available in a few minutes," Feisty tells me. "You can discuss the pros and cons of stitching this up, and if you'd like to see a plastic surgeon. But you'll probably get sent to ophthalmology to rule out internal damage to your eye."

"Sounds about right." It's consistent with what Louise said before she'd shipped me off to the hospital.

Feisty snaps her gloves off and tosses them into the trash. She heads toward the door, then halts and turns around. "You know, Mr. Daughtry, you have a nice face. It would be a shame to see you back here with it all busted up again over someone who didn't return your feelings."

"Yeah. I know." I admit it.

"It's none of my business, but you don't want to be with someone who's hung up on somebody else." Her expression is a compelling mix of concern and vulnerability as she nods at me. "Trust me."

"What's your name?" I ask.

"Zoe."

"Thank you, Zoe. For everything."

"You're welcome, Mike." Without another word, she flings back the curtain and leaves the room.

ZOE

"I'm sorry, Zoe." Macy squeezes my shoulder gently. From my barstool perch behind a carved oak support beam, I watch with train-wreck horror as my boyfriend slithers onto a seat across from the beautiful woman I'd just met.

What is he doing?

Tim twists the chair at an awkward angle, blocking Louise's escape path. She keeps her face neutral, but her posture is far from welcoming. Tim doesn't seem to notice though. Or maybe he just doesn't care. He leans across the table with his best attempt at a seductive and persuasive smile.

"So… I guess it's safe to assume that Louise and Tim know each other?" I ask.

"Yeah, it is." Macy sighs, then sits on the barstool

7

next to mine. "Louise and Tim were together. They broke up about a year ago."

So that's her.

"I had no idea it was Louise. Or even another nurse." Every time we talk about the future, Tim gives me this sob story about how his ex screwed him over and he's "just not ready yet".

"Zoe, I didn't know that you and Tim were seeing each other, or I would have warned you about him."

"Warned me?" The words croak from deep in my dry throat.

"Yeah." Hesitation flickers across her face. "They met in the ER. Right after Louise moved here and started her job when Tim had about a year left on his surgical residency."

"Sounds familiar." I take a long slow gulp of my Sazerac before going all in. "Tim told me that he was a wreck after she broke up with him. Do you know why she did?"

Macy gives a loud snort of disgust. "Zoe, Louise broke up with Tim *after* he told her that he wanted to date other people. Apparently, he wanted to try his luck dating as a high-paid doctor. Louise finally told him to fuck off. About damn time, too. The rest of us were done with him long before that."

"The rest of us?" This part I'd never heard.

"Tim changed after his residency. For some weird reason, he was an asshole to every one of his friends from before. He's mellowed out a bit in the last year, but he's not a popular guy. Don't take my word for it though. I'm biased. Ask around."

"Well, that explains a lot."

"Like what?"

"Like why he waited until the last minute to decide about coming here with me tonight." He didn't want me to mention it to anyone else who knew him. "And why he didn't want me to tell anyone at work we were seeing each other."

"Or why he didn't tell you he already knew me or Paul? Or that his ex would be here?" Macy shakes her head. "He didn't tell you any of that either, did he?"

"Nada."

"Well, Christ. This is awkward." Macy folds her hands on the bar.

"Just a bit."

My attention drifts back to Tim and Louise. I can't hear what they're saying, but suddenly Tim looks furious. Louise stands to leave, and Tim grabs her arm. A strange mixture of disgust and sadness sinks deep into the pit of my stomach.

"Oh, no. He didn't." Macy comments on the same scene. "Who the hell does he think he is?" She curses and stands but I reach out to hold her back.

"Macy, who is that guy?" My chin tilts toward a tall, super-fit man beelining his way toward Tim.

"That's Usalv." A slow smile of satisfaction transforms Macy's face. "Louise's boyfriend."

"Shouldn't we do something?"

"Get the popcorn."

"Oh Jesus." I'm humiliated that Tim's behaving this way toward someone else when he's here with me. I'm disgusted at the way he's treated me and the people here tonight. But mostly I'm angry at myself for being so stupid.

For liking him. For believing him. For trusting him.

As Usalv inserts himself between Louise and Tim, part of me hopes that he kicks Tim's ass. But Tim is smarter than that. After a heated exchange, Tim gets up and retreats from the table. I'm both grateful and disappointed that I couldn't hear their words over the other conversations in the bar.

"Well, that was quick." Macy sounds disappointed, too.

As Usalv sits down in the chair vacated by Tim, Louise pats his forearm in a soothing gesture. It becomes clear from all the way across the room that they've entered their own bubble, oblivious to everyone around them.

An odd mixture of jealousy and irritation overwhelms me at the sight of them together. Content, happy and satisfied. All states of existence that forever evade me.

"Careful," Macy warns, reading my thoughts. "None of this is Louise's fault. She lives with Usually now. And even if that weren't the case, she's been over Tim for a long time. Louise isn't your problem. Tim's your problem."

"Not anymore." I swirl the rest of my Sazerac around the bottom of the glass before finishing it in a single gulp. "Thanks for the party, Macy." The zipper of my purse gives a shrill sound as it opens, and I reach inside to pull out a twenty-dollar bill.

"Hey, I got this round." Macy stops me. "Don't worry about it."

"Thanks." Anything that speeds up my departure makes me grateful right now.

"Hey, are you sure you're okay?" she asks. "Can I do anything for you?"

"Actually… I think you've done enough. Thanks for the drink. And for the heads up."

"I'm so sorry, Zoe."

"Me too, Macy. Goodnight." I turn and leave before the tears in my eyes start flowing down my face.

MIKE

As THE ARCHED ENTRYWAY TO O'SHEA'S LOOMS AHEAD, my decision not to hammer down large shots of top-shelf whiskey fills me with regret. But I know showing up drunk at Paul and Macy's party would be a spectacular display of bad taste and judgment that won't be forgotten or forgiven anytime soon.

Not only would Paul and Macy take turns booting my ass while the other one chewed it, looking like a pathetic loser in front of Louise and Usalv is a shit role I'm tired of playing.

As I pace outside the entrance, the streetlight glints off the etched-in digits of my Girard-Perregaux watch. It's after eleven, well past fashionably late and too early for the party to be over.

Fuck... Is it too much to hope that everyone I want to avoid is gone now?

Probably.

A gentle breeze with a familiar dose of humidity

gusts through the evening darkness. My dislike for sticky air, combined with a strong desire to get this evening over and done, propels me toward the entrance.

Say hello to the family. Avoid... them, *but let them see you're here. If they talk to you, tell them you're meeting someone and leave. Be polite. And casual. But whatever the hell happens, don't mingle or have more than two drinks. Out in thirty minutes, tops.*

"Sorry," says the owner of a tearful voice as she pushes the door open and runs straight into me at full throttle.

"That's okay," I reply. Her chin is tucked into her chest, but there's something familiar about the bright blue highlights streaking through her jet-black hair. "Shit night?" I ask in an irrational attempt to cheer her up.

"You have no idea." She looks up at me and my mouth goes dry.

Her eyes are coal black, framed with impossibly thick glossy lashes too delicate to be fake. Blue eyeliner and champagne-colored eye shadow frame those ebony pools, making her eyes look surreal.

"Oh, I might surprise you." I give her a sympathetic smile.

"I should go."

"Have we met?" As soon as the words are out, they sound like a cheesy pickup line.

"I don't think so," she replies and breaks eye contact. "Good night." The high heels of her black sandals strike the pavement as she walks to the curb where she stops to check her phone.

It's a testimony to my sorry-ass state of mind that I

can't remember where and when this striking woman with the chic offbeat style crossed my path. Frustrated, I stare after her retreating frame. My brain is going into overdrive when a man bursts out the door and races down to the street after her.

This douche I know. Suddenly it all clicks into place. Doctor. Hospital. Nurse. Zoe.

"What are you doing?" he asks the woman standing by the curb.

"I'm leaving." She snaps her phone shut and walks away. "Get away from me."

"Just calm down." He rakes a hand through his sandy brown hair. "I'll give you a ride."

"Did you even hear me?" She stops and turns back toward him. "I don't want a ride. I'm not going anywhere with you." Her shrill voice becomes calm. "We're done, Tim."

"You really need to calm down."

"You really need to get lost." Her hands fly to her tiny waist. "How could do that to me?"

"I did nothing to you." Tim sounds impatient.

"On top of everything else, you're going to stand here and lie to my face? You used me as an excuse to come to this party and hit on your ex. You didn't tell me she'd be here, or that you and the hosts despise each other."

"You're making a big deal out of nothing," he scolds her. "We were just talking. As far as crashing this party, they're having it at a bar, okay? It's not in a private place —anyone can just walk in. So I didn't crash it."

"No. I won't stand here while you tell me I'm overreacting after you pawed that woman until her date showed up. You embarrassed me and made me look like a fool in front of people I work with. Now goodnight and goodbye."

She turns her back to walk away, but Tim catches up quickly and grabs her arm.

"Let go of me."

"Just hold on."

"Let her go, jerk-off," I call from the door of the bar. "Right now."

"Mind your own damn business," Tim barks at me without turning around.

"That's not gonna happen." I approach the street and stand about six feet away from them. "Now you either let her go, or you can try to do something about it."

As Tim turns, a flash of recognition crosses his face.

My response is a curt nod of acknowledgment.

Yeah, asshole. It's me. The one who kicked your ass before.

A few years back, Louise had brought him to the St. Patty's day parade with the crew. When the men and women had separated, he'd gotten a little too graphic about his sex life. Being somewhat drunk myself, I'd punched him. Thanks to inconsistent accounts, the police had declined to arrest me. After that, Tim had tried to sue me, but my lawyers were better and my pockets were deeper.

Whatever move he makes he will lose. And he's smart enough to know it. The only question is whether he wants to be publicly neutered or try holding on to a woman who doesn't want him anymore.

"This is fucking ridiculous," he says, releasing Zoe's arm. "You're on your own. Bitch." Without another word or a backward glance, Tim disappears down the street into the night.

As his footsteps fade into silence, I watch as Zoe heaves a big sigh of relief.

"Thank you," she tells me in a detached voice.

"Don't worry about it." I bury my hands inside the pockets of my pants. "I wasn't hitting on you back there, you know. We have met before. In the ER. You helped patch up my eye a few months ago. It's Zoe, right?"

"Mike." For a moment, Zoe smiles. "You were hard to recognize without an ice pack covering your face. You look good." She flushes. "I mean, your eye looks like it healed okay."

"Yeah, it's fine now. Thanks." I study her troubled expression. "Hey, are you okay?"

"I will be." She glances up and down the street. "I just need to figure this out."

"Figure what out?"

She sighs. "I sure as hell don't want to go back in there." She tilts her chin at O'Sheas. "I don't want to go home. And I don't want to be alone right now."

Zoe's feelings mirror mine exactly. It's clear from her fight with Tim that Louise is still here with Usalv. And as much as I love Paul and his wife, I don't want to deal with them right now either.

"That about sums it up." I reply. "There's a boutique hotel a few blocks from here, with a really nice bar." My thumb flips over my shoulder toward Hotel St. Rafe. "Would you like to get a drink?"

"I would love that." She looks visibly relieved.

"It's a walk." My gaze shifts down to her high-heeled sandals. "Do we need to get a cab?"

"Actually, a walk sounds good."

I pause a moment and wait for Zoe to catch up. When she reaches my side, we walk down the street together.

ZOE

"I didn't realize this even existed. Thank you for bringing me here." My voice sounds sweet and slightly slurred, even to me.

"You're welcome. This is one of my favorite places in the city," Mike says.

"Mine too. Now."

My fingers slide the ankle strap of my sandal down and off, and the black high-heeled shoe drops onto the tile floor with a hollow clap. With the naked toes of my bare foot, I remove my other shoe. The cushy modular couches make it easy to get comfortable, and I tuck my legs up underneath me.

The open-air bar on the roof of Hotel St. Rafe hums with an energetic buzz of music, conversation, and alcohol. Top-shelf alcohol. It's time for me to taper off, but I really don't feel like it.

"Zoe?"

"Mmm?"

"Would you like another?" Mike asks when the waiter approaches.

"Sure."

"Another round, please," Mike tells the waiter.

"Thank you," I say.

A slow smile forms on Mike's lips as he watches me. "I have happy memories of this place from when I was younger."

"Tell me," I encourage him.

"In college. This was my favorite hotel and bar. Sometimes we'd sneak up here just for the view. We'd try to order drinks, we'd get a little loud. Then someone would usually complain and get us kicked out."

I follow Mike's gaze as it skates across the city skyline. It's clear and dark tonight. A beautiful gold crescent moon hangs in the sky like a fine pendant necklace.

"Good for you. I didn't do nearly enough sneaking around when I was young. It's one of my biggest regrets." It's sad to hear out loud, but it's the truth.

"Really?" Mike sounds shocked. "That's a surprise."

"Why?"

"I don't know." He cradles that dimpled chin in his palm and studies me. "The bright blue hair. The piercings. The way you dress. It just screams rebel."

"What's wrong with the way I dress?" That his opinion matters so much takes me by surprise.

"Nothing." He gazes at the halter top of my jumpsuit. It's blood red with dark swirls of blue that match my hair —and one of my favorite outfits. "It's a bit... exotic. But it really works for you."

"Thanks."

Mike gives me a peculiar look, but the arrival of our drinks distracts him. He takes his from the waiter's tray and swirls it thoughtfully. When the waiter offers me mine, I remove it and take a large sip.

"Well, if being a rebel means defying convention, sure," I admit. "But for some of us rebelling is just an attempt to keep our lives from being flushed down the crapper. It's not really a social cause or conscious choice."

"What were you rebelling against?" he asks after I set my drink on the end table next to me.

"Life as I knew it. My mom was a single parent who had me at nineteen. I never knew my dad, who left right after I was born." I fold my arms around me. "Lather. Rinse. Repeat. Five years later the same thing happened, and my baby sister came along."

"Wow," Mike finally mumbles. "I can't even imagine."

"Being poor sucked, but that wasn't the worst part." The words rush out as I attempt to eject the panic that fills my core. "The worst of it was watching my mom fritter her life away. Hoping and waiting for our dads to do the right thing. She lost hope. She stopped trying to make things better and settled for how they were."

"And you wouldn't settle?" Mike asks.

"For the life she had? No *way*. So yeah, call me a rebel if you want."

"It suits you." He sounds pensive. "How did you end up being a nurse?"

"My spectacularly unspectacular public high school had a hookup with a local university that gave me dual credit and a scholarship for nursing. My four-year degree was done at twenty-years-old. At twenty-one, I had my license." I raise my glass in a quirky salute. "They saved my life. Who knows where I'd be without them."

"To public education." He raises his glass and clinks it against mine.

"Amen." We laugh in unison for a moment.

"Sorry," I say. "It's the absinthe talking. Didn't mean to be such a downer."

"You're not a downer." He bites his lower lip. "That's the last thing you are."

"Ambivalent compliments make me think too much. And it's hard to concentrate right now." My body shudders as a strong breeze slides over me, giving me a moment of clarity. "So tell me, what are you rebelling against, Mike?"

"Me?" He seems surprised by the question. "Nothing."

"Come on. No one who says they want to be an MMA fighter when they grow up seriously means it. At least no one past the age of twelve." Our eyes meet and we hold each other's gaze. "What's up with that?"

Now it's Mike's turn to swig half the contents of his glass in a single gulp. The air is hot and sticky, which makes our premium cocktails glide down easy.

"Win or lose, it's all on you," he explains. "I guess that's what drew me to it. You're matched to an opponent by size. As you get better, so do your opponents. Whatever comes out of it, nobody else can say they gave it to you. Nobody can whine about you having some unfair, intangible advantage."

"Quite the rugged individualist, aren't you?"

Mike shrugs, but his smile fades. "Something like that."

Instinct tells me not push it. Instead, I smile before laying my head on the cushion of my chair and staring into the clear night sky. It's hard to tell what's more intoxicating—the drinks or the views.

"Another round for the two of you?" I look up at the waiter's question.

"Zoe?" Mike asks.

"No thank you," I reply.

"We're done tonight. Thank you." Mike tells the waiter.

"Shall I bring the bill, Mr. Daughtry?"

"No. Put it on the room."

"Of course, Mr. Daughtry."

I watch hazily as the waiter retreats, trying to process their conversation.

"You...have a room here?" I ask.

"Yes."

"You're staying here?"

"Yes." Mike hesitates. "I... know someone who's in real estate. When they need help showing properties on weekends, I stay at this hotel. It keeps the bills paid."

It's weird he hadn't mentioned it before. But then again, why would he? "Well, it's getting late, and I've got a long way home. This was nice. Thank you."

"You're welcome."

"Can I at least pay for my drinks?"

"Don't worry about it. It's all going to be expensed," he assures me.

I'm struggling to say something that doesn't sound stupid or silly, which is really hard when it's this late and you've had as much to drink as me. But then Mike speaks and leaves me completely speechless.

"You can stay here tonight. If you want," he announces in a pass-the-salt kind of tone.

My eyes widen in response, but he cuts me off. "It's got two queen beds. You can just crash. Leave whenever. It's up to you."

"Oh."

He shrugs at my noncommittal response. Then he pulls out his wallet, removes a plastic keycard and tosses it on the table. "Room 10223. In case you decide to stay. If you don't, just drop the key off at the desk."

"Okay." I give him a shaky nod.

He stands and smooths down his long-sleeved shirt before planting a gentle kiss on the top of my head. "I enjoyed our evening together. Good night, Zoe."

"Good night, Mike."

He gives me a slight nod then turns and leaves, strolling toward the building entrance, leaving me alone with my empty glass in the humid darkness.

"Hello?" I rap lightly on the door. When there's no answer I slide the keycard into the reader under the doorknob and enter the dimly lit hotel room.

The door opens into a tiny foyer beside a closet next to the bathroom. Across from the entry, the closed curtains of the large windows filter the light from the city skyline.

"Mike?" I call into the darkened room.

The only sound that reaches me is that of heavy, forced breathing. When I follow it past the entry hall to its source, my own breath hitches.

On the nearest double bed, Mike lies spread eagle with the covers thrown back. He's stripped down to a pair of gray boxer briefs, and any doubts I harbored about him being a full-time athlete dissipate then and there.

He's perfect.

Tall without skyscraping. Muscular without being overly ripped. A series of exotic script-like tattoos run across the width of his arm underneath the shoulder, sparking curiosity without being a distraction.

I sit on the side of his bed and trace the curves of his tattoos. When Mike stirs, I shake him gently.

"Mike?" My voice is just above a whisper.

Mike's gray eyes open and he bolts straight up, grabbing the hand I have on his arm.

"Zoe?" He sounds puzzled.

"Hi."

Mike glances at the bedside clock. "Where have you been?" His speech is slurred with slumber.

"Trying to sober up and go home. Epic fail." I'm distracted because our hands are still touching. "Can I stay with you?"

"Sure. Come here." He slides his big body over and makes room for me.

"What—?" Before I can protest, his muscular arm

snakes around my waist and pulls me onto the bed next to him with the fluid ease of a child picking up a stuffed toy.

"Ssh," he murmurs into my ear. "It's okay. Sleep now."

My tired brain tries to explain that I wanted to stay in the same room, not the same bed. But as I curl up my body on the warm mattress where Mike laid, and he settles the large comforter over both of us, weariness overcomes me.

"Sleeping now," I tell him before drifting off.

MIKE

I TRY TO ROLL ONTO MY STOMACH, BUT THE FIRM ROUND
ass pressed snugly into the curve of my groin stops me.

"Zo-Zoe?" I rasp at the woman sleeping beside me.

She responds by burrowing deeper against me,
resting her head on the crook of my arm. With Zoe lying
so close, it's impossible not to study her face. Her nose is
small, her lips are big and cherry red. Her skin is milky
white and flawless with a tiny hint of pink.

Beautiful.

As I attempt to remove my arm out from underneath
her, that pretty face turns into my chest. The halter top
strains against the back of her neck, leaving a red mark
on the delicate skin. She winces, then tugs the snap
closure behind her neck open. The front of Zoe's jumpsuit pops open like it's spring loaded.

Oh, damn.

She's wearing a strapless, little lace bra that's taped
to the skin underneath her arms. The breasts they cover

look firm and well-shaped without being too large. As I resist the urge to touch them, other parts of me swell.

"Zoe." This time my voice is louder.

She wakes with a start. As she rises off me, her halter top drapes down past the super-flat stomach and the tiny waist. To make matters worse, Zoe doesn't realize it.

"I… uh need to use the bathroom." I stare at the TV screen on the opposite wall while my free hand balls into a fist underneath my pillow.

"Oh. Oh!" She looks down at herself and snatches the sheet to cover her nearly naked front. "Sure." She slides off me quickly. "Sorry."

"It's okay." I roll out of bed before Zoe notices what she's done to me.

"I need to wash up when you're done," she says.

"The shower and sink are separate from everything else. You don't need to wait."

"Okay. Thanks." As she scoots to the edge of the bed and fumbles with her top, I head quickly past the sink and two-person shower before entering the throne room and sliding the door shut.

In private, I bury my face in my hands.

Christ.

Much as I'd like to blame this whole escapade on too much booze, the fact is I didn't drink a helluva lot last night. Nothing before the party where I never showed up. Back here at the bar, it was just three mixed drinks. Okay, they loosened me up a bit, but it takes a lot more than that to put me out on a bender.

Outside the door, Zoe pads across the floor. She

curses loudly, then turns on the water beneath the large mirror overlooking the sink.

I smack the space between my eyes a few times in a lame attempt to shake the morning haze. When it doesn't work, I sigh in disgust.

Even without beer goggles, the fact is that I like Zoe even more than yesterday. How the hell often does that happen, especially in a situation like this? We can't stay here, with her sweet cakes spilling out everywhere and me trying like hell to keep my hands off.

No, that would not be a good idea. We'll get dressed, leave, have something to eat. Then I'll get my car and take her home.

Good plan. I finish up and slide the door open.

"Zoe?" When there's no answer, I assume she's gone back to bed. Can't say I blame her. I'd love to join her, but that's not a good idea right now.

I slide my shorts off and pad over to the two-person shower, fling open the door and step in. That's when I realize the sound of water running is coming from the shower.

Our shower.

"Holy Christ." My voice is low, raspy whisper.

Zoe stands under the powerful stream of the far shower on the interior wall, with her head fully submerged under the pummeling jets of water. Her back is turned, giving me an unobstructed view of her full, fine round ass and the tiny waist that sits above it.

"What the hell are you doing in here?" I shout when my voice returns.

"Me?" Zoe gasps and turns around, giving me a full-frontal flash as she covers her mouth. "I thought you were in the bathroom!"

"I called out to you. When you didn't answer I thought you went back to bed."

"That's because I was in here. Didn't you hear the water running?"

"It's a hotel, Zoe. There are probably five-hundred people trying to take a shower right now. Guess I tuned it out."

My eyes absorb the now naked breasts and well-toned stomach. Try as I do, it's impossible to look away. I roll my lower lip inside my mouth and bite down hard on it. Zoe follows my gaze and throws those tiny hands around her critical bits.

"You should have told me you were going to shower." My voice quiets.

"I wasn't awake yet—oh shit. Ow!" A large blob of shampoo streaks into her eyes. Zoe tries to rinse it out without using her hands, opting to keep her body covered. It's a total fail, and she continues to curse and groan. I come to her aid, guiding her into the shower stream and using my hand to direct the water toward her eyes.

"It's okay now," she tells me, pulling my hand away from her face.

By now, our naked bodies are touching. Zoe's soaped-up breasts press against my front, our arms entangled around her neck and face.

"Zoe?" I'm mesmerized by the water running over the cherry-red lips of that x-rated mouth when she stretches up on her toes and kisses me.

I've held myself in tight check since last night on the roof, but after this, well, self-control heads straight to hell in a handbasket. I grip both sides of her face, bringing her lips to mine, while my groin swells to full-sized action mode.

"Zoe," I choke out between kisses.

She replies by sliding her hands up along the planes of my chest.

"Hey. Zoe." I grasp her collar bones, hesitating to move. "I'm only human, okay? If you're planning to stop, do it now. Please."

She moves her head away from the shower stream, looks directly into my eyes, and shrugs. "I'm... I'm not going anywhere, Mike. If you want to stop—"

"No, I'm good."

"Then don't talk." Her hands descend the curve of my spine and beyond. "Just..."

"Just what?"

"Let it happen."

I mentally ransack the room and my things in it before I blow out a sad breath. "There's only one problem."

"What?"

"I don't have any condoms." Things have been tame for me, lately. The box in my bedroom nightstand at home has been untouched for months.

She bites her lower lip. "I do. In my purse on the sink. Be back soon." Without another word, she turns and walks through the large shower door.

While she's gone, I scrub myself all over with the open bottle of shower gel. I love bars but hate how they make me smell the day after. Sweaty. Boozy. And some-times even smoky, depending on your crew. By the time I'm done, she's standing next to me in the shower, watching with a pleased smile.

I return her smile and hold out my hand. She shakes her head.

"I'm on hormonal birth control, but I like using a back-up. It's a female condom."

"A, a what?" My fingers wring the hair at my neck.

"It goes inside me. And *you* go inside it." She sighs, then smiles patiently. "Just make sure your aim's good."

"Not a problem." My voice is sober and serious. "Never has been."

She giggles and I can't help but laugh too. It breaks the tension and uncertainty. Zoe brings her quivering fingers to her cherry-red lips and kisses them gently. Then she runs the pads of her fingers from the base of my throat, over my chest, down my abs...

...and down, down, ever downward...

ZOE

THAT WAS A ROTTEN THING TO DO TO MIKE.

I drag tense fingers through the wet wavy strands framing my face as I look out the bus window and sigh audibly. It's a long ride home to Belmont-Cragin, and it gives me time to face facts and figure things out.

After our...encounter in the shower, I had headed into the bathroom and disposed of the condom. That's where it hit me that I didn't want to see to Mike and pretend it had never happened, or try to be casual, or discuss meeting up again when we both knew it was bullshit.

Instead, I'd wanted to get the hell out of there. Right *then*.

With my clothes, shoes, and purse by the sink, it was easy to dress quietly and leave while Mike did the same as he waited for me in the bedroom. I did my best to muffle the sound of the door opening before practically sprinting to the elevator.

Way to keep things classy, Zoe.

My temples throb, but it's difficult to say whether it's a hangover or guilt. I've never done a one-nighter before. Never *ever* thought it would happen.

But then again, going back to Tim isn't something that's ever happening, either. Last night I made sure of that. Tim would never get back with me if he found out, and I'm too much of a straight shooter not to tell him if it ever comes up.

There's no regret, except for not seeing Mike again. He seems like a great guy. It would've been nice to give it a real go with him. But I know he was trying to unload some heavy baggage himself. Hopefully, last night got him past it, too.

Tears well in my eyes, but I brush them away quickly. It's best to just forget about it now and move on.

Thank you, Mike. For everything. I hope I helped you, too.

I t's about a ten-minute walk from the bus stop to my house. The familiar dull beige brick bungalow comes into view, and I reach for my keys as I turn up the path to the front door. My hair is mostly dry, and with any luck, it doesn't give away the circumstances of my earlier departure.

"Well, that's quite the walk of shame you've got going on there."

And yet another hope evaporates into the ethos before noon today.

"Thanks, Mom. Good morning to you, too," I reply while removing my key from the lock and shutting the front door behind me.

Mom sits at our rectangular dining table. It runs along the wall of our kitchen. Dark under-eye circles make her look tired, which is probably the case. My mom works as a bartender on weekends, and she doesn't get home until after three in the morning. That she's up before noon on a Saturday means something's on her mind.

"Where's your sister?" she asks.

I jerk my head back at the question. "Didn't she spend the night at Lola's?"

'I don't know." My mother scowls at me. "Did you check on her?"

"No." I throw my keys on the end table and try to collect myself. "I told both of you there was a work party downtown and I wouldn't be home until morning. *You* should have checked on Chloe."

"I was working last night."

"So was I, until about seven thirty." I scroll through Chloe's text messages. "All I have is that she's spending the night with her friend. That was right around when school ended."

"I got that one, too."

"Then you know what I know. Why didn't you call her?"

"We're not on the best of terms at the moment." My mother sighs. "Thanks to all this college stuff."

"Oh, so now this is my fault?" I feel the familiar feud coming on.

"Well, she's not home, so now's as good a time as any," she replies.

"Okay." I press my fingers against my temples. "But I can't have this conversation without coffee. Is there any left?"

"Kitchen counter. Same as always," she grumbles in her this-isn't-over tone.

"Thanks, Mom."

I take a deep breath, walk past her, enter the kitchen and inhale the welcome smell of my mother's coffee. She still uses an old-fashioned percolator. It's the one thing she makes that is truly delightful.

Coffee sloshes onto the counter as I fill my favorite mug and top it off with hazelnut-flavored creamer. I grab the tired white towel hanging from our oven to wipe down the counter before heading out to the table.

"What's on your mind?" I take the chair across from her.

"I don't like this college idea for Chloe. It worked for you, and I'm glad it did. But... Chloe's not like you and I don't want to put her through this."

"Mom, Chloe will graduate high school. *Without* getting pregnant. She needs to have a plan for after." We've had this argument before, and it's not one my mother will ever win with me.

"I saw how hard you worked to get through." My mom shakes her head at the memory. "It was a goddamned nightmare."

"A goddamned nightmare?" My blood pressure surges. "No. A goddamned nightmare is watching you trying to raise two kids on a never-ending series of dead-end jobs and unstable income. Screw that."

"Watch it," she warns me.

"I'm sorry." I raise my hands in surrender. "I don't mean it disrespectfully. I know you did your best." Tears well in my eyes for the second time this morning. "But I'm not going to pretend that it wasn't a nine-year-old's version of hell just to make you feel better. Or let you railroad Chloe. She's smart enough for college. The rest she'll just have to gut out."

She wears a look of hopeless desperation that ignites a primal childhood fear. "You were incredibly motivated and driven about school. That's not Chloe."

"Um, no." I'm not a frightened kid with no say in how my world works anymore. Never, ever again will I be that uncertain or helpless. "I was incredibly motivated about not living hand-to-mouth. If the way out had been tap-dancing or telepathic fortune telling, I would've been motivated about those things instead."

"But even with your financial assistance and scholarship, you had to take out loans." My mom slams her coffee cup on the table. "I don't want to see Chloe have a hard time and drop out, then have to pay back a bunch of money for nothing. Or have her credit flushed down the toilet."

"Mom." I set my cup on the table. "My scholarship and financial aid covered all my school expenses. I took the loan for living expenses because I couldn't work during the semester."

"Exactly," she replies. "If you couldn't do it, Chloe

sure the hell can't do it. She'll need to take out loans.
And that scares me."

"Chloe won't have to borrow as much. She might not
need to borrow at all if you and I keep our jobs and she
gets the same deal I did. But she must live at home, just
like me."

"She should just start working and try to save some
money up," Mom insists.

"Doing what?" I exclaim. "She won't get paid
enough to save unless we give her a break on living
expenses. If we do that, I want to know it's leading
somewhere."

"You're still paying back your loans," she reminds
me quietly.

"Yes," I admit. "Over three years I borrowed twenty
thousand to cover rent, food, transportation and living
expenses. It should be paid off by next Christmas. I
could do it faster, but then I wouldn't have savings.
Chloe will be fine, Mom."

"It's too much responsibility." Mom jumps up from
the table. "I can't let her do it."

"Then what's your plan? How long do you think I'm
going to stay here and keep paying the lion's share of the
bills? What if something happens to me? Or I move out
and get married? Then what?"

"Are you getting married?" Her eyes brighten.

Oh *Lord.*

"No! And that's not the point." I jump to my feet
now. "Even if she only gets a two-year nursing degree,
once she has her license, she'll always be able to work

for a decent wage. Part time, full time, night time. Whatever."

"I don't know." She turns away, swaying back and forth. "I need to think about it more. Could you please call your sister and tell her she needs to come home? The car's out back."

"You want me to go pick her up?" I ask.

"If she needs a ride. That would be great."

"Sure." I grab my cell phone and head into my bedroom.

"Zoe?" Mom calls after me.

"Yeah?"

"Were you with the doctor last night?"

My head droops against the inside the door. Out of sight, I bang it several times against the worn oak finish. "No, I wasn't. And Mom?"

"Yes?"

"You…should forget about the doctor. It didn't work out."

"Oh, no!" she exclaims. "How could you screw up like that? What did—"

I slam my bedroom door, cutting her off. Then I dial my sister.

"Hey," I say when Chloe picks up.

"Hey, Zoe. What's up?" she answers.

"Are you at Lola's?"

"Yeah."

"Okay. You need to come home now. And Chloe, can you do me a favor?"

"Anything."

"Next time, tell Mom where you're at. I'm catching all kinds of crap because you told me and not her."

"Sorry, Zoe. I guess I thought I told her, too."

"It's no big deal. Just for next time, you know?'

"Sure. Can you come get me?"

"Of course. See you soon," I tell her.

"Thanks. Love you, sis."

"Love you, too."

MIKE

WHAT A *SHIT-SHOW*.

In normal circumstances, I'd have avoided Macy and Paul like the plague after ditching their party. But when Zoe snuck out of the hotel room like a thief Saturday morning, there was no other way for me to track her down. Part of me still thinks I should let the whole thing go. Someone doesn't leave like *that* if they aren't gone for good.

Then I had found it. One hundred-twenty dollars in wadded up bills that she had left on the bathroom counter. WTF?

Did she pay me for... sex?

One, that's pure bullshit. And two, if she'd wanted to compensate me for my contributions to her evening's entertainment, I'm worth way more than fucking one hundred twenty.

Determined to set Zoe straight on this, I call Macy on the pretense of apologizing and try to get her talking about Zoe. First comes the post-apology rant. Then my query about who had been there, which naturally leads to the inevitable play-by-play on Usalv and Louise.

"Louise?" I ask Macy. "You think I want to know about Louise?"

"Well, don't you?" she replies.

"You can't tell me anything. She's with Usalv now. I got it." Awkward sad silence. "So, anyone else from the hospital there?"

"Few of the docs from my shift. Most of the nurses and—oh! How could I forget to tell you?"

"What?"

"Tim Mazure showed up. With the new nurse, Zoe, I'd invited. She had no fucking clue."

Now that news sets my jaw on edge. "What do you mean, she had no fucking clue?"

"Zoe didn't know what we all thought of Tim. Or that his ex was at the party," Macy rants. "Do you know that asshole tried to hit on Louise before Usalv showed up? In front of Zoe. In front of everyone."

Christ. "That's messed up. Have you talked to her since?"

"No, I won't see her until later this week."

"Don't the two of you work together?"

"I'm Tuesday, Wednesday, Thursday plus two Sundays. She's Monday, Tuesday, Wednesday, with two Saturdays a month. So sometimes, but not every day."

The outcome of that conversation is me standing here outside the hospital entrance at eight o'clock. It's a pleasant summer evening, still with plenty of daylight accompanied by a warm breeze. The lively evening atmosphere provides a stark contrast to Zoe's exhausted-looking frame as she exits, wearing bright blue scrubs with a heavy backpack riding on her shoulder.

"Zoe?" I call to her as she approaches the sidewalk.

When she recognizes me, those tired liquid black eyes spring to life. Her forward momentum stops and she looks around for a split second before squaring her shoulders. "Mike? What are you doing here?"

"Not stalking you." I raise my hands in surrender. "I promise. But we need to talk after what happened, and the only real-world thing I knew about you was that you worked here."

"Did it occur to you I left that way because I didn't want to see you again?"

Damn, that stings a little more than I'd like. "Yeah, it did. But then you paid me, and that I couldn't let go."

"I paid you?" She looks confused.

"A hundred and twenty. For the best time of your life."

"You think I was paying you for, for—" She chokes back a laugh. "For real? That's what you thought?"

"Wasn't it?" Why else would she leave me money?

"No. God, no." Zoe walks up to me and stands on her tiptoes. "And just so we're clear, that was *not* the best time of my life."

"Ouch." I reach around her waist and whisper down into her ear. "Come on though, seriously. It was at least top three, right?"

Zoe drops back down on her heels, eyes rolling like monster truck wheels. "Tell me something Mike. Was that your best performance ever?"

"What?" It would be a total lie for me to deny that I'd love another go at her.

"How about top three?" Zoe throws me an expectant look.

"Hey, wait a minute!" I call after she resumes walking down the street.

"Judge not that ye be not judged," she replies without stopping.

"Can we go somewhere and talk about this, please?" I ask after catching up with her.

"Sorry. Can't." Zoe checks her phone. "I'll miss my bus."

Bus? "How about I give you a ride? We can talk on the way."

Her pace slows. "Where's your car?" She looks tempted.

"Wherever the hospital valet parked it. It shouldn't take too long."

"You valet parked your car?" She shoots me a peculiar look. "Isn't that expensive?"

Damn, she gets preoccupied with the weirdest shit. "It beats wasting my time being lost."

Zoe shrugs it off. "A ride would be nice. But I live far away."

"I don't mind." It's the truth. "Where do you live?"

"Belmont-Cragin," she replies. "Addison and Cumberland."

"By the golf course?"

"Yeah." She seems surprised. "Do you live near there?"

"No. But my real estate job sends me all over town." I touch her shoulder blades as I steer her toward the valet station. "Come on. Even if the valet is busy, it's still faster than the bus. And lots more comfortable."

Zoe stands over by herself, waiting quietly until the valet brings my car.

"Uh... nice car," she comments while the valet holds open the passenger door of my bright white full-sized luxury SUV.

It's clear she's got some kind of hang-up about money, but I don't want to turn her off. My desire to put Zoe at ease makes me do something that causes instant guilt and regret.

I lie to her.

"Thanks. It's a company lease car I use for showing properties. It should have been turned back in, but I didn't get over to the office today. Lucky for you."

"And that's not a problem? You won't get into trouble?"

"Not really." Now that's true because the car is mine, while the 'office' is my family's business. And if my sister Janet is around, which is all the time these days, I avoid it like the Black Death.

We're silent as I pull the car out into traffic. Zoe's eyes are closed, and her head is tilted back against the seat rest. She looks exhausted. As eager as I am to continue our conversation, it breaks my heart to disturb her now.

Instead, I flip the radio on to my favorite stand-up comedy station. Listening to jokes while driving around keeps me grounded. As I brace myself for the Eisenhower Expressway, Zoe springs to life, laughing with me at the same punch line from the comic on the radio.

"Good morning," I joke with her. "Didn't get a chance to say that before. Not my fault though."

"Nope. Not your fault," she replies sans apology.

"Okay, Zoe. I have to ask now because it's been bothering me all weekend and today. What the hell were you paying for when you left me money, and how did you decide that one hundred and twenty covered it?"

"Drinks. It was to cover the drinks," she tells me in a matter-of-fact voice.

"What? No, that's bullshit. We discussed the bar tab that night. I told you not to worry about it. I'd expense the fucking drinks." I snap the radio dial to the off position. "Don't treat me like a brain-dead moron. I remember everything about that night, including how many times you cried out when you came." My voice is calm and cool. Like ice.

There's a stilted silence in the car after that, which is fine with me. I'd rather we not talk than listen to Zoe lie.

"I left you all my money, because I didn't want to see you stuck with an obnoxious bar bill or any extra room charges for me staying there." Her voice is calm and cool. Like ice. "We both know MMA doesn't pay your bills, and I didn't want you to get jammed up over me."

"There's no way I'd let myself get jammed up over something like that."

"Trust me, Mike. Rich guys are assholes. And the rich guy you're working for is probably one."

Her words stun me like a sucker punch. "Wait... what did you say?"

"Rich guys have no real-world worries, so you never know from one day to the next what they're going to have a problem with—or who."

"But money's not all bad, is it?" I recall what she said that night about growing up poor and struggling to go to college and get a job as a nurse.

"Money itself? Hell no. Who doesn't need or want money? But men with money think they're god's gift. And being with one…can be like having another full-time job."

"How?" Heat creeps up the back of my neck.

"You're never thin enough. Or pretty enough. Or impressive enough to their crew, or grateful enough he's with you. Never mind the not-so-subtle hints about how you're so replaceable. Whatever. Hashtag get bent."

Sweat beads up under my clothes. It's getting hot in here. And not in a good way.

"Hey, what are you doing?" Zoe asks as her window opens.

"Sorry," I tell her, soaking in the coolness of the outside air. "There's some crap on my side mirror that's making it hard to see." Another lie, which is becoming a habit where she's concerned. Even I know this isn't good.

"After Tim, you couldn't pay me to date a guy with

money. My mother would shoot me for saying that, but hell no."

"Tim Mazure isn't that wealthy. He's a surgeon," I insist. "Maybe what you think you know about rich guys is tainted by a bad example. And not a very accurate one."

"Oh, so you're saying more money would make a guy like Tim less arrogant? Yeah, sure." She laughs then pauses. "Hey, how did you know Tim's last name? Or that he's a surgeon?"

Oh *shit*. The last thing I need is her asking that douche or his crew about me.

"Um, I don't know," I reply with stilted calm. "You must have told me that night at the bar."

"Really?" She throws me a skeptical look. "Are you sure about that?"

"How else would I know?" I *must* stop lying to her. But when?

"Make a right up here," she tells me.

We ride along in silence for a few minutes until she points out a tiny two-bedroom brick bungalow in the middle of a block of pre-war houses. I pull alongside the curb and shut off the engine. Zoe makes no move to leave. Instead, we stare out the window at the tired looking tiny house when I hear myself speak.

"Why d'you leave like that?" As soon as the words are out, I know that's the real question that's been eating me alive since Saturday. "I didn't mistreat you, and unless you faked it, you had a fantastic time." I draw an audible breath. "Did you fake it?"

"No. I didn't fake anything," she admits. "But I've

never done that before, and when it was finished…I
needed it to be over."

"Never done anything like what before?"

"Slept with a stranger. Gone to a hotel with someone
I'd just met." Her delicate fingers cover her mouth. "It
should have never happened."

"So I'm a mistake?" My core fills with quiet
hostility.

"No. I made a mistake."

"Okay. But it happened."

"Yes, it did. And you are a reminder of my bad decision and judgment. And people like me don't have the
luxury of making big mistakes." She shakes her head
and gazes out the window at her tiny house. "We lack the
resources to recover from them."

I swallow hard. "Do you regret it?"

"I'm not sure."

"What the hell does that mean?"

"It means it's too bad we didn't meet under different
circumstances. But we didn't." She clicks the lock on the
door and opens it. Then she checks her phone quickly for
messages. "My sister's home. I need to go, Mike."

"Wait." I gently pull the phone from her fingers.

"What are you doing?" she asks but lets me take it.

I punch my number into her phone, then wait for
mine to ring. When my pants pocket shakes, I hang up
and give it back to her.

"We're not bad people," I tell her. "Both of us were
in a place that wasn't good. We didn't hurt ourselves or
anyone else. Call me?"

"Maybe."

Without another word, she hops out of my car and walks up the path to her front door, leaving a hole in my soul.

ZOE

It's nine-thirty at night as the front door shuts with a dull thud, and I snap the deadbolt into place. It smells like something burned. Hopefully, enough of it is salvageable for dinner because I'm starving.

"Zoe?" my little sister calls from the kitchen.

"It's me, Chloe." I throw my backpack on the ground. "Is Mom home?"

"No, she's working." Her tone is filled with resignation.

"I'm sorry you're here alone so much. It's just damn near impossible for me to get home any earlier than I do."

"It's okay. Besides, my school financial stuff got here today. It's not the same as what you told me. Can you take a look? *Before* Mom?"

It's Wednesday night, the end of another brutal week for me. I'm exhausted, hungry and just want to go to bed. But if there's something wrong with Zoe's scholar-

ship money, it's better that I find out about it
before Mom.

"Sure. Is there anything to eat?"

"Sort of. I tried to make a chicken casserole, but I
burnt the topping." She looks squeamish. "The bottom
tasted pretty good though."

"I'm sure it's fine. Let me heat up a plate and I'll
meet you in the living room with your school
paperwork."

"It's on the coffee table," she replies. "I'll get you
some dinner."

"Thanks." I collapse onto the couch and pull a sheaf
of papers out of a large document-sized envelope with a
familiar university seal on the front. "What's the
problem with these?"

"You know how you told me the program was free
when you attended?"

"Yeah?"

"Well…" She pauses to place a plate on the table and
sit next to me. "… it says here that the student responsibility is eight thousand dollars for year one." She points
to a column of numbers. "How can that be?"

What the hell?

"Chloe, bring me your schedule for last semester,
and for the upcoming fall semester," I tell her after
speed-reading through the packet.

She hurries back with two almost-transparent pieces
of goldenrod colored paper. It takes me less than a
minute to study them and conclude what I already know.

"Do you see these classes that don't have asterisks
next to them? These aren't part of the program require-

ments. They are recommended courses for the nursing program."

"I know," she replies. "The high school counselor told me to take them. We were both afraid that if I got bad grades in the nursing courses, I wouldn't get into the college program." She takes a deep breath. "I'm not as smart as you, Zoe. We both know it."

"We can argue about that another time." I sigh and toss her class schedules onto the table. "The problem now is your prerequisites won't be completed by high school graduation. This eight-thousand dollars is the estimated university tuition for those courses, which aren't free."

"Oh, no." Chloe covers her mouth. "Mom's going to shit a cinder block."

"She'll do worse than that." I rub my throbbing temples. "She won't sign any paperwork if it means you taking on that kind of debt. And that includes your high school schedule."

"My schedule? Why not?"

"You know most of these courses are through the community college?"

"Yeah. So?"

"Well, normally there's a tuition charge. We don't pay it because of Mom's income." Thank god my nursing salary isn't part of that mix.

"But if we don't pay, why wouldn't she sign my schedule?"

"Because it includes a financial agreement. Mom agrees to pay tuition if you become ineligible for financial aid, which happens when you take classes outside of the program. She won't sign if you need to take on debt."

"Why?"

"Because she thinks this whole college thing is a big scam, and that this program is nothing but bait and switch. And she won't change her mind."

Chloe gives a thoughtful nod. "She's never liked the idea of me attending college even though I know she's proud of you." She shakes her head. "Why doesn't she want that for me?"

"It's not you. A lot of people… like us attempt college. They need to borrow money but quit or flunk out with no way to pay back all they owe. It ruins lots of people." The cords in my neck constrict. "And then there's me."

"You? What did you do?"

"I'm twenty-three years old. I still live at home. I don't have a man in my life or any children. Add to that I'm still paying loans back, despite my full tuition scholarship."

"Do you regret it?"

"Hell no. Both our dads left. Mom not having a good, stable income didn't stop that from happening. But her having one might have prevented other things."

A familiar haunted look appears on Chloe's face as she stares past me into space. "Zoe, I don't want to live here forever, and I don't want my only way out to be hooking up with a guy."

"Then for god's sake, Chloe, have a plan. And if you don't like the one that worked for me, then come up with something else. But don't expect the things you want from life to just *happen.*"

She nods. "What should I tell Mom?"

"Nothing. Tell her I looked everything over and it's fine. She just needs to sign it."

"But what about the eight thousand dollars?"

"Don't worry about it." I swallow hard. "You won't have to borrow. I'll take care of it."

"Are you sure? That's a lot."

"I… have some savings." I struggle to hide the disappointment in my voice. "It should be fine."

Chloe releases a relieved sigh. "Thank you, Zoe." She reaches across the couch and gives me a deep hug. "I didn't know what I would do."

"You can always tell me stuff. You know that, right?" I promise.

"Yeah. Thanks, Zoe."

"Anytime." I give her one last squeeze before pulling out of her embrace. "I'm beat. It's been a long week, and it's time for me to crash." I peel myself off the couch. "You good for tomorrow?"

"I'm good." Chloe studies me. "You okay?"

"Fine," I reply. "Goodnight, Chloe."

"Goodnight."

Without another word, I close my bedroom door quietly behind me.

~

I lean my rigid shoulders against the door with my eyes shut tight. When they open, I try to soak in the sanctity of my room. It's small, but it's the only thing I have that's truly all mine.

"Are you sure you want to spend your money that way?" Mom had asked.

"I'm sure."

To my surprise, it was the first and last time she'd raised the subject.

Gramms died about six months after I finished nursing school, leaving Chloe and me to claim our own space in the tiny three-bedroom, one bath house we all called home. The bedroom we'd both shared was in better shape, so we all agreed Chloe would keep our old room; Mom would move into Gramms', and I'd fix up the room vacated by Mom.

The seafoam colored-paint that Chloe helped me apply to the walls, the double-sized antique brass bed I'd found at the resale shop, and the modern driftwood colored desk I'd splurged on all amount to the most money I'd ever spent on just myself. Except for school.

I stand up straight and let out a groan of pain, exhaustion and frustration.

My sore back reminds me of what a long and tiring day it's been. I strip naked, and toss my scrubs and underwear into a wicker laundry basket.

I remove the fuchsia-colored cotton robe hanging from its wall hook and put it on. Then I walk over to my tiny gray wooden desk and remove an envelope stamped with the university seal from the thin flat top drawer.

Fuck. I had plans for that money.

I collapse onto the tropical-colored comforter that covers the antique brass bed, and stare at the framed photographs of the ocean on the far wall. I've never had a real vacation, at least one where we've gone far away.

"Are we going to see Uncle Phil and Aunt Kaye, Momma?" I'd asked.

"Yes, Zoe."

"When, Momma? Can we go right now?" seven-year-old me pleaded.

"Not now, darling. July fourth, same as always."

Mom's brother and his wife moved to the Wisconsin Dells after they got married. Every summer without fail, Gramms would pack up our ancient Subaru wagon and take us to stay with them during the fourth of July. Aunt Kaye worked in a hotel, but Uncle Phil gave boat tours, and we'd come along for free. Back then, it had been my idea of heaven.

Then Uncle Phil and Aunt Kaye had divorced, and we'd stopped visiting on July fourth.

Besides the Dells, I've never really been anywhere. Holidays are when bartenders make the most money so during those times Mom worked, we'd stay with Gramms.

Are the sky and water really that color somewhere? The photos on my wall make me wonder. But now it will be even longer before I can see for myself.

Fuck, I had plans for that money.

Being an emergency room nurse wasn't my first choice, but it paid the best of all the other options, and I needed money. But the work and pace are back-breaking, and after about a year, it's clear I can't do it forever.

My acceptance letter taps out a desperate rhythm on my naked knee.

I've always wanted to work in Obstetrics and Gynecology, in a clinic or private practice that helps adolescents with pregnancy prevention and STD education, among other things. Because I'd avoided all those things and graduated high school with options, I'm much better off than any sane person would have predicted.

I had planned on starting the Advanced Practice Nurse Practitioner program this fall. They have part-time admission, and the savings I've scrimped together would cover my own expenses. But Chloe needs her first college degree more than I need a second one.

An audible whimper escapes from me, and I wipe a single tear away with the envelope corner. When my vision clears, I stare transfixed at the ocean photographs again.

Someday, I promise myself.

Someday, I insist.

And somewhere deep inside me, hope gives way to weariness.

MIKE

"YOU GOT THIS, MIKE. YOU GOT HIM!" DOUG TELLS ME from ringside.

About damn time, too.

Drew's a scary-ass Muay Thai style striker, with hands and feet equally fast and dangerous. It's taken me the better part of two minutes to set up this takedown, and he's been kicking the shit out of my shins all the way through it.

"Shake him off, Drew," Doug coaches from ringside.

No chance. Drew's on the ground, and I'm on top in the mount position. He tries to protect his body from my punches by tucking his arms in tight.

That leaves his throat wide open.

I grab it with my right hand. Drew tries to protect his throat, but he lifts his elbow when he grabs my hand. Once that happens, an armbar is easy from this position. Drew struggles for a few seconds, then taps out.

We exchange a clap on the back and stand, each at our own pace.

"Great job, guys," Doug tells us. "Damn Daughtry, you're on fire today."

"Thanks, Doug." It's nice to hear, especially coming from him. He's a fitness and conditioning coach who's big into Muay Thai. Doug works with a lot of guys here, and everyone thinks he's great.

"Have you considered going down a weight division?" he asks. "It might work out really well for you."

"That's a good twenty pounds," I reply. "Not sure if I'd be much of an opponent once I got there."

"You'd be fine. Besides, you'd only need to make the weigh-in." Doug shrugs. "Think about it."

Doug turns to Drew but stops mid-sentence when he realizes Drew's distracted.

"Earth to Drew," Doug teases. "Hey, where you at?"

"What?" Drew answers, leaning toward us but keeping his focus elsewhere.

Doug follows Drew's gaze and draws in a breath. "Oh… I see." He whistles. "You know her?"

"Not yet," Drew confesses.

"She looks a little corporate for me," Doug says. "But things can change. I've always had a thing for redheads."

Corporate? Redhead? Oh fuck.

Not her. Not here.

My back is to the entrance, so I glance over my shoulder to see the distraction in action. It's her. Janet. My older sister. And if she's gone to the trouble of tracking me down here, she's probably pissed off about something, which is never a pretty sight.

As I spin to gauge the distance between here and the men's locker room, Janet spots me and makes eye contact.

Don't even think about it, her hazel-green eyes telegraph.

I turn back toward the guys and take a deep breath, waiting for the click-click sound of her designer pumps to reach us.

"Hello," Janet says dismissively to everyone after reaching the ringside. Then she whispers to me, "We need to talk."

"Well... hello." Doug eyes her up and down. "I'm Doug. And you are?"

"Not interested," Janet tells him with an icy smile.

"Your loss, Red." Doug's voice becomes indifferent.

"My name's not Red," Janet informs him between gritted teeth.

"Then what is it?" He gives her an expectant look.

"I'm not telling you my name." She crosses her arms over her sleeveless white blouse.

"Suit yourself, Red." Doug crosses his arms. "But we're in the middle of training here, and we need to get back to it."

"She's my sister. Ease off, okay?"

"Your sister?" Doug sounds surprised. "She's got way better legs than you, dude." Doug studies Janet's thin muscular legs under the straight nude colored skirt she's wearing.

"Oh, please," Janet growls.

"You have no idea," I reply to Doug, who's half-flirt-ing, half-serious. "Twenty-some years of ballet."

"It had to be something like that." Doug nods. "You still dance, don't you, Red? When you get the chance."

Janet remains silent but nods firmly.

"Good for you," Doug tells her. "Never give it up."

"Never," she assures him.

"Janet, this is Doug, one of the coaches, and Drew, my sparring partner."

"Nice to meet you, Janet." Doug smiles and extends his hand. "I'm Doug."

"Yeah. You said that already." Janet reminds him. "So did Mike."

"That's all right. I've got no problem with you knowing my name." Doug's hazel eyes soften.

"I'll remember it now," she promises.

"Well, I hope so."

"Um, this is Drew." I steer Janet's attention away from Doug.

Drew reaches a hand toward her. "Hello."

"Nice to meet you," she responds, shaking his hand quickly. "I need to speak to Mike. It's kind of impor-tant," she announces to all of us.

"Sure, Janet." I'll even agree to an ass-chewing to avoid watching Doug's trainwreck style of flirting with my sister. "We'll just go hang out over here. Thanks, guys." I toss my gym bag over my shoulder and steer Janet toward the hallway.

It occurs to me that I haven't even cooled off from my sparring session with Drew before Janet's intrusion. When we reach the end of the corridor, I remove the clean white towel stored in my bag and wipe down my head, face and arms. When I'm done, Janet greets me with an expression of impatient disgust.

"I can't imagine why you prefer this place to work."

"I know you've never understood, or been too interested in trying to, but this *is* my work." Experience tells me the best way to deal with Janet's hostility is patient calm.

"That's what we need to talk about," she insists. "And since you won't come to the office, I've come here."

"What's the problem?"

"The problem? The problem is that I've been working my ass off," she hisses. "I don't know what deal you worked out with Dad about this MMA bullshit and your office-casual attendance policy, but damn it, neither one of you asked me, and I'm done with it."

"Done with it? I thought you were happy running the company. We all know it suits you. You'll be CEO when he retires, and I've got no problem with that. You'll do great." Janet's made it clear from the get-go she wants the top job. Well, it comes with baggage.

"Great? I'm drowning here. *I'm* Chief of Operations now. Dad plans to retire from his CEO position in the next few years. You need to get ready to step into my old role or we need to explore other options."

"Other options?" This is new.

"Bringing someone in from the outside."

"If that's what you think we should do…" It's never good to argue with Janet while she's on a roll.

"Michael." When she uses my full name with that

scathing tone, bad things are happening. "You'd need to give up your corporate salary."

"What?" Now she's gone off the rails. "Why?"

"We can't pay two six-figure executive salaries and get only one executive." She makes an open-handed gesture. "And the caliber of person we need won't be free or cheap."

"You want to cut me off?" She can't do this.

"No. What I want is for you to show up at the office and handle the commercial leases." Janet folds her arms. "You were always so damn good at it. You have a knack for knowing what business will work where. I don't know why you gave it up for…for whatever this is."

"I still do corporate leasing. It's not fair for me to lose my salary."

"Michael, the work you do is great. You just don't do enough." She sighs. "Anyway, I didn't come here to argue. Just to give you a heads up."

"A heads up? About what?"

"I'm letting you know this is the direction I want to go with the company. Since you're never at the office, I'm done hoping you, Dad, and I can have a casual conversation about this. Instead, I'll bring it up on the fourth of July."

"Well, you two can discuss it if you like. But I won't be there."

"What do you mean, you're not coming?" Janet blinks hard, almost like she's recovering from a physical slap. "Mom and Dad expect to see us all together, three times a year. Christmas, Easter and the fourth of July."

"I've made plans to travel this year. I'm sorry."

"Do they know you're not coming?"

"I haven't told them yet." The thought of leaving hadn't occurred until a few moments ago.

Janet gives me a frustrated groan. "Fine. That's fine, Mike. But you know what? Dad and I will have the conversation, with or without you. If you don't want to be there, that's your choice."

"You won't get an agreement without me there." My resolve is firm.

"We'll see about that," she says through gritted teeth.

"Janet," I address her calmly but forcefully. It stops her in tracks. "You should know that Dad agreed to this 'MMA bullshit,' as you like to call it, because he didn't want us at each other's throats. And yes, I have a talent for leasing and operations. One you lack, to be honest. If I come back, it won't be to work for you. So be careful what you ask for."

"I'll see you when I see you," she replies after a stunned silence.

Without another word, Janet turns around and heads toward the exit.

God *damn* it. She will not ruin my holiday. It's time for me to get the hell out of Dodge. I rustle through my bag and pull out the cell phone from its dedicated pouch. Zoe's number pops into my contacts screen.

Meet me at St. Rafe's. Please. I text.

ZOE

"Name, please?" a man wearing a hotel blazer asks me at the terrace entrance of St. Rafe's.

"I'm meeting someone," I explain.

"Name, please?" he repeats without looking up from the seating chart at the hostess stand.

"Daughtry," I tell him.

"Mike Daughtry?" He looks up at me with suddenly undivided attention.

"Yes. Do you know if he's here yet?" I ask.

"I can have someone check for you, Miss...?"

"Inglot. Zoe Inglot."

"Right away, Ms. Inglot." The host calls over a waitress and whispers into her ear before she disappears.

While they go to see if Mike's arrived, I study the light-filled lobby of the restaurant. The black-and-white checkered marble floor combined with the vivid still-life pictures on the tan walls give the place an elegant but easy-going vibe. Behind the hostess station, a painting

with a crowd of people sitting around a long table dominates the room with its silent cheeriness.

It reminds me of how much I like this place even
though I've been here only once.

"Ms. Inglot? Mr. Daughtry is outside on the terrace.
This way, please." The host gestures toward a double
French door that leads outside.

It's late Sunday morning, and it's crowded with
people enjoying brunch. Who can blame them? It's clear
and sunny without being too hot yet, and they fill the air
with laughter and happy chatter. Just like the picture.

The long trip across town didn't thrill me, but I
wanted to see Mike again. After our last…encounter
here, I felt badly about the way it ended. He's too likable
to be treated like that.

Then he turned up at the hospital, intent on trying to
get past it, too. The thought of seeing him again fills me
with tense excitement. Is it possible to put that behind us
and start over?

I'm led past the crowded tables, around a terraced
wall with pink and red flowers growing out of a long
planter along its top edge. Behind the terrace are two
tables with seating for four. The first one is empty. The
second is occupied by a fit tall blond man dressed in
casual clothes. He's turned away from the aisle as he
studies the killer view of the city skyline.

"Mike?" I say.

His blond head snaps around. "Zoe. Nice to see
you." He stands and there's an awkward pause as we
muddle through how to greet each other before he plants

a quick kiss on my temple and gestures toward an empty seat across from him.

"Wow, you lucked out this morning," I tell him.

"How's that?" he asks.

"This table has a great view of everything, and it's not crowded here at all. How d'you manage that?"

"Just lucky, I guess." He shrugs. "Would you like something to drink? Coffee? Mimosa?"

"Yes, please—" I'm trying to decide when Mike does it for me.

"Two coffees and two mimosas, please."

"Right away." The man disappears.

"You look good," he says.

"Thank you." I smooth my chambray colored T-shirt dress over my thighs and let him push the chair into the table. "So do you."

"Thanks." Mike removes his dark sunglasses and tosses them on the table before resting his hands on both thighs. "How is everything?" he asks.

"Fine. Work is going okay." Our conversation feels awkward. "How about your MMA stuff?"

"I'm at a crossroads," he admits. "One of my coaches suggested I drop twenty pounds and fight in a different division. I'm thinking it over."

"Oh," I reply after a long pause. "Is… that what you wanted to meet me about?" It doesn't make any sense.

"No. I want to ask you something." He crosses his legs while keeping his hands on parked on those athletic thighs. "But I don't know how you'll react."

"Well, maybe you should just ask and find out." My

palms sweat and I smooth the skirt of my dress to dry them.

"Good idea." He smiles at me with perfect teeth. "Zoe, have you ever been to Mexico?"

"Mexico? No. I've never been anywhere, really." It's hard to hide the regret I feel about it. "Why do you ask?"

"You remember me saying I work in real estate part time?"

"Yeah. So?"

"The, uh…company gives out a prize for most annual sales." Mike grabs the sunglasses from his empty salad plate and twirls them in the air by the nose bridge. "This year I won."

"Congratulations!" I'm truly happy for him. "It's nice when something good like that happens."

"Yeah, it is."

"What d'you win?"

Mike stops spinning his sunglasses. I can see the lenses are blue, and that the amber-colored frames are a near perfect match for his hair. "A trip to Mexico," he answers softly.

Is he serious? What kind of company does that?

"You know, I've heard about people winning stuff like that. But I've never met anyone who did. That's fantastic." I smile at him.

Mike's stoic expression surprises me.

"What's the matter? Don't you want to go?"

"Oh, I want to go all right." His gray eyes meet mine. "And I want you to come with me."

My first response is laughter. Knee-jerk nervous laughter. "Me? I can't."

"Why not?" He sounds genuinely puzzled.

Thank god the waitress arrives with our drinks, giving me much needed time to collect myself. She seems a little nervous as she removes two flutes from her tray and places each one in front of us. When that's done, she sets down a tray with sugar packets and fresh cream before slowly pouring coffee for us from a large white carafe.

"Can I take your order now?" she asks.

"We'll order food later," an impatient Mike replies. "Leave the coffee, please."

She leaves the carafe, then walks away. Mike watches her retreat for a few seconds, then turns back to me.

"So where were we?" he prompts.

"Mike, I can't afford to take a trip like that. And I won't let you pay for it."

"I'm not paying. I won it, remember?"

"I don't have a passport." Hopefully, my embarrassing confession ends the conversation.

"Do you have a birth certificate?"

"At home," I admit.

"Good. There's a business center in the hotel. We can do the application and run to the drugstore for a photo. Let me do the rest."

I take a deep breath and reach for my mimosa. It's cold, sparkling and delicious. It goes down easy, most in a single gulp.

"Would you like another?" he asks with an amused expression.

"Please don't try to make me drunk."

"I'm not trying to get you drunk. I'm trying to get you to relax." He eyes the nearly empty flute in my hand. "We both know it'll take way more than two of those things to get you anywhere close to drunk."

There's a measured silence as Mike tears open a pack of artificial sweetener and pours it into his coffee cup. Then he stirs it, the spoon clanking a regular rhythm against the ceramic cup.

"Mike, I know why you're asking me, which is why I'm saying no."

The clanking stops. Mike brings the cup to his mouth and drinks before setting it down. "Really. And why's that?"

"What happened the last time we were here." I gaze across the skyline before looking back at him, "it's not a regular thing with me."

"I know that," he replies with quiet resolve. "We've already had that conversation."

"Then why me? Why not a friend or someone you know better?"

Mike shrugs and drops his hands onto the tabletop. "I didn't plan to mention it, but since you brought up, then let's be honest about it. Fair enough?"

"Fine."

"I don't want to spend the fourth in Chicago, or with anyone else I know. I want to spend it with you. And it's not a given, but if we do end up horizontal we both know things are good on that front, don't we?"

"Not a given?" I ignore his last question and shoot him a doubtful look.

"No," he insists. "There's plenty to keep us busy if

we choose to avoid the bedroom. Swimming, water-skiing, para-sailing, snorkeling. We can even hire a boat to take us out on the ocean—"

"—the *ocean?*" My heart rate spikes and my palms bead with sweat again.

"Yeah. You like the beach, don't you?" He sounds unsure for the first time this morning.

The *ocean.* "Where is this place?"

"Punta de Mita. Just north of Puerto Vallarta. On the Pacific coast of Mexico..."

Mike continues his description, but I'm not listening as I stare out over the city skyline at Lake Michigan. The ocean? Before I'm thirty? Travel to a foreign country? Never thought it could happen.

This is crazy.

I barely know him. And yet...we have this attraction that's hard to deny and even harder to ignore. I had been rebounding the night we met outside O'Shea's, and Mike hadn't given me the impression he was in a happy place either. It hadn't mattered that night if I liked him. In fact, it would have been better if I hadn't.

But I had. And I do. If Mike had asked me to someplace less exotic, say the Wisconsin Dells, would my answer be no? Then why should it be no now?

"... unless you have other plans." Mike's question brings me back to the present. "Do you?"

"No. No plans. Mom's working and Chloe plans to hang out with her friends' family." Wow. It wasn't until just now I realized I'll be alone if I don't make plans of my own.

"The holiday falls on a Thursday," he tells me. "We

can leave before it or after, depending on your work schedule."

"I'm done on Wednesday that week."

"We'll take the first flight in the morning. We'll be on the beach by early evening. Still plenty of light." Mike reaches over and caresses my forearm as it rests on the chair. "I won't lie. The jungle is miserably hot this time of the year, but hell, so is Chicago. The villa's right on the ocean and it cools off at night. The place is air-conditioned—"

"Yes," I blurt, cutting him off.

Mike stops talking. He looks surprised, then very pleased. "Good. I'm glad."

"Me too," I reply. It doesn't make much sense, but it feels… *right.*

He nods with a pensive look on his face. "Let's finish here and get to work on that passport application."

"Right." I grab his untouched mimosa and bring it to my lips with a smile.

MIKE

"THANK YOU," I TELL THE HOTEL STAFF AFTER THEY finish setting up our late night dinner on the dining table of our ocean-front suite.

They smile and leave quietly. When the front door closes, I stroll to the open wood-and-wicker doors that lead to the deck of our zero-edge swimming pool.

Zoe's lithe body floats in the lighted water as she clasps the edge of the pool and stares out at the Pacific Ocean. It must be close to nine as the sunlight dwindles across the horizon in vivid color.

My intent was to call her in when dinner arrived, but looking at her now, mesmerized by the last few moments of sunset, I grab two Topo Chico mineral waters from the mini-fridge and rejoin her in the pool.

"How's it going?" I descend the steps and walk through the water to where she lingers at the edge.

"Hey." She gives me a lazy, tired smile. "This is great. I can't believe I'm here." She takes the sparkling water from my outstretched hand. "Thank you." The crack in her voice tells me she's not just talking about the drink.

"Glad you came. Take this, Zoe. You're not drinking enough."

"I am thirsty," she admits. "The humidity catches up fast."

"Plane rides are also very dehydrating. Drink up," I insist.

"Really? I didn't know." She brings the bottle to her lips and takes a long sip.

Oh god. That plane ride. Any lies I've told her should be atoned for with that journey all the way from Chicago to Puerto Vallarta in cargo class. It was so fucking tight that the tiny Yaris cab we took to the resort felt like a luxury vehicle.

It had occurred to me to try to upgrade to business class and tell Zoe that it was all part of the package, but I was afraid to push my luck. Thank Christ she's on the tinier side because I'm a big guy and if we hadn't shared our leg room, I would've needed to be shoe-horned and wheel-chaired out of that miserable window seat.

It was worth it though. Zoe had never been on an airplane before, and she took it all in like an excited child. She had listened intently to the emergency instructions, double-checked her seatbelt, and asked to hear the entire list of beverages. For the first two hours, we'd talked non-stop and then I nodded off. When I woke, her chin was propped up on my chest and she was staring out the window. She'd been like that the whole time.

Still, though, I need to work on my cover story for an upgrade on the return trip.

"Dinner's here. Do you want to change before we eat?" I ask.

Zoe looks down at her new purple bikini. "Yeah. I'll just take a quick shower and be right out."

"Hurry. The lobster's getting cold."

"Uh-oh!" she replies and breast strokes to the stairs, drink still in hand.

I watch with excitement and admiration as she climbs the pool stairs and toddles into the suite, her fine, firm, well-sized ass looking fabulous wearing the six-hundred dollar bandeau bikini I'd purchased for her from the hotel boutique, along with two matching cover-ups and another one-piece suit.

She'd freaked out about how much it cost, so I told her everything was in pesos and really cheap as I handed the clerk my Black Card. She'd looked great in everything and judging from her other clothes, doesn't splurge on herself very much.

A pang of guilt hits me like a tidal wave, but this time, I force myself to shake it off.

Get over it, I tell myself. *Enough with the nickel and dime shit. I just want her to be happy and have a nice time. There's nothing wrong with that.*

But I'm not quite convinced as I wade to the stairs and head into the suite.

∽

"Three lobster tails?" I marvel. "That's impressive, Zoe."

"Is that a lot?" she asks. "I must have been hungry."

"It's not *that* much." I smile.

"Sorry." She looks embarrassed. "I've only had lobster once before. And it wasn't this good."

"Don't be sorry." It upsets me that she feels self-conscious. "You should be hungry. It's been such a long day. I'm surprised you didn't crash hours ago."

"I wanted to. But I waited to see how the full moon looked over the ocean." She leans back in her chair and finishes an ice cold bottle of Dos Equis while gazing out over the ocean. She's so peaceful, so at home here.

Getting the Daughtry Capital Development Corporation, or DC-squared, to take an ownership stake in a luxury ECO resort had raised eyebrows when I pitched the idea. Janet worried about the cap rate on the property. In the end, it was Dad who got her to agree.

Part of the early phase of development had been the sale of a few villas to private owners. I'd loved the place so much that I'd purchased this villa out of my private funds, separate from the business.

This is my villa.

I come here at least twice a year, more if life allows it. As I watch Zoe's tired, excited eyes, it's hard for me to hold back from telling her that this place she's so fond of is mine. I want to hear her say it was a good choice... and that she'd even come back here with me someday.

But we can't have that conversation now, and it's something I regret.

"Come on. Let's go back outside to watch the moon and water." I stand and hold my hand out to her.

"Okay." She smiles and gets up, half-asleep.

We approach the near edge of the pool where Zoe pulls up the hem of the light green cotton dress around her thighs and sits with her feet in the water. My gray workout shorts make it easy for me to do the same beside her. When I'm seated, she covers my hand with hers.

"This has been a wonderful day. I can't thank you enough."

"Well, I'm glad you could come with me."

We sit there in silence, looking out over the coastline at the gentle ripples of the ocean. The moon is full and its pale yellow light glistens off the crests of the waves.

"We should go to bed soon." I squeeze her hand. "We've got a huge day tomorrow."

Zoe stiffens, and I realize how my words must have sounded to her.

I clear my throat and continue. "We're booked for snorkeling after breakfast and sailing in the afternoon. We eat lunch at the hotel's beachside restaurant." When she says nothing, I talk faster. "Depending on how you feel, we can go into Puerto Vallarta in the evening."

"That sounds great." Zoe withdraws her hand from mine and folds it over her knee. "Thank you for doing all this." Her eyes never leave the horizon.

I get it. This is a test.

Before we get to tomorrow, we've got to get through tonight. I made a promise to her before we left that there wouldn't be any pressure once we arrived. If I make a move on her now, I'll get shut down for the rest of this trip, maybe even for good.

There's no way in hell that's going to happen.

"Which bed do you want?" I ask. "They're both king beds, but the master is obviously a larger room. I'm good either place."

"I'll take the smaller room," she replies. "It's closer to the pool and I might swim in the morning before breakfast."

"If you prefer, we can order room service." I stand up at the side of the pool. "But we should be at the beach by eight-thirty."

"No problem. I'll be ready."

"Good night, Zoe."

She looks at me for the first time since we came outside after dinner. "Good night."

Without another word, I turn and enter the villa.

ZOE

HE'S SO...*HOT*.

Mike emerges from the crystal clear waters of the ocean, straight out of a casting call for the latest super-hero action flick. His wet swim trunks cling to obscenely muscular thighs and the drawstring waist gaps down from his ripped abs, exposing the well-defined ridgeline of his hips.

I bite my bottom lip as memories of what lies below his waist confront me.

When I'd agreed to come here, my major worry had been putting off his advances until my feelings became clearer. Watching him trek up the beach toward our private canopy, his tan lines accentuating the golden glow of his skin, I realize it was the height of deranged stupidity to feel that way.

He's super fine and knows it—you can't look that good and *not* be aware. But the thing about Mike is that he doesn't acknowledge it. Just watching him come up the beach, two attractive bikini-clad women smile and say something to him. He nods, smiles back and keeps going. Because he *knows* he doesn't have to work for it. Eventually what he wants will come to him.

Me included.

"Hey," he greets me, then throws his snorkeling gear on the ground by the canopy entrance before diving onto the long white couch perpendicular to mine. "You going back out?"

"Not right now. I've got sunburn on my back."

"The sun here is brutal." He lies back on the couch. "Are you using the sunscreen?"

"By the gallon. But I either missed a spot or it's not working well."

"There's aloe vera gel on ice in the cooler." He pulls the cooler off a nearby table and removes a bottle containing clear gel. "You want it?"

"Yeah," I reply. "Thanks."

I squeeze a blob of gel into my hand, then slide it underneath my kaftan toward the uncomfortable burning sensation. When one spot remains out of reach, I shift awkwardly, wrestling with myself underneath the kaftan. Between my unsettled movements and groans of frustration, I catch Mike watching from the other couch.

"You need help?" He's propped up on his elbow with an amused expression.

"That would be nice," I admit. "I can't reach the spot on my back that's burning."

"Well, if you want, I can rub the aloe on your back."

"Sure. There's just one problem."

"What is it?"

"I'm naked under my kaftan."

"Naked?" Mike's voice is cautious and controlled as he studies the curves underneath the gauzy fabric. "Um, why?"

"The straps were rubbing against my sunburn and it was painful. It was clear I was done for the day, so I stripped it off and just wore the kaftan instead."

"Well, I'm okay with it if you are." He gives me a casual shrug.

"I'm good. Just give me a minute." I take one towel from a pile of several clean white ones that were here when we arrived and wrap it firmly around my waist. Then I spread another out on the rough outdoor fabric of the couch before lifting the kaftan over my head.

My naked front faces the thick fabric wall of the tent. Behind me, I hear Mike fumble with the ice inside the cooler. As I smooth down the towel on the couch, Mike's indrawn breath makes me freeze.

"Wow… uh—I mean, ouch." He takes a deep breath. "That burn looks bad."

"Damn it." As I settle onto the couch, I reach under my stomach and loosen the now-uncomfortable knot at my waist. "I'm ready, Mike."

He doesn't answer and there's an awkward pause before an ice cold sensation sends pleasant shivers down my spine. Mike rolls the frigid bottle of aloe across my lower back, but in this heat, the cool doesn't last long. There's a pregnant pause between the throaty *gluck gluck* of the thick gel being dispensed and the moment Mike's cold hands touch my heated flesh.

"Ahh," I hiss as the cold gel stings before it starts to soothe.

"Easy," Mike says.

When I relax, Mike smooths the gel along the surface of my skin. My whole back is tender, but now the sting of the aloe vera exposes where the sunscreen worked and where it didn't.

"We should have left sooner. I'm sorry, Zoe."

"Don't be. I didn't realize I could get burned like that so quickly. Next time I'll know. Every single minute was amazing."

I'd never been snorkeling before, and I'm an okay swimmer. But Mike loves it and swims like a marine mammal. He's also stronger and fitter than me, and much more comfortable diving deep. At first, he'd tried to take me with him, but I'd felt guilty for holding him back. So I waited on the surface of the water, face-down and back exposed to the sun, watching for him.

"Did you get to see much from the surface?" His hands skate across a layer of slick gel on my lower back, rubbing tenderly as he speaks.

"Plenty. There were lots of bright-colored fish, the lobsters near the rock formations. But even just the undersea landscape was just so, so…"

"Calming?" His palms still on my back for a moment.

"Exactly."

"How about the manta ray? I tried to point it out to you, but wasn't sure you'd see it from so far away." The massaging resumes.

"Oh, I saw it all right." I remember feeling relieved when Mike resurfaced. "That was not relaxing."

"Nothing to worry about. I wasn't that close to it, either."

Mike squeezes out more aloe gel, letting it act as a balm on my skin. Then he waves his hands over it, creating a cool breeze that amplifies the soothing sensation.

I sigh and relax, stretching out on the long couch.

A lingering silence ensues as Mike rubs my back again. His strong fingers take their time, moving in long sensual strokes. He explores the curve of my lower spine, sliding his hands slowly over my flesh. Despite trying to remain still, I feel my body become aroused by his caresses, and I arch into his touch while his fingers travel along my skin.

He seems to sense my struggle because he stills before removing his hands. I hear the *gluck gluck* of more gel being squeezed.

"The back of your legs are red, too." He tells me in a stilted voice. "You want me to put some there?"

"Okay." I sound detached, even sleepy.

Mike smooths the gel along my naked calf, resuming his clinical strokes. He bends my leg and rubs the front before his fingers find the shallow depression behind my knee.

"Ahh," I cry out, surprised at my reaction. I squirm, straighten my legs, then curl my back toward him, displacing his hand to my lower thigh.

With a firm hold of my inner thigh, he keeps my leg bent, and caresses the back of my knee like a cello master. Mike's touch is a mixture of gentle strokes and pulses of pressure from the pads of his thumbs. Who knew being stroked there could be such a turn on?

"Mike…"

"Zoe?"

There's a certain challenge in his voice. He *knows* what he's doing and how it makes me feel. It's that ever-present smug confidence, a familiar effect in the bedroom since our first time together. My eyes shut tight, and images from the hotel room at St. Rafe's come flooding back to me.

The cold stone of the shower wall against my back. Mike's forehead pressed under my navel, pinning me against the wall. Exploring every inch of me with his tongue as the water rushed over us, the heated steam making it difficult to breathe.

Damn it.

I've greatly underestimated my own attraction while overestimating my self-control. Despite knowing him only a short time, recovering from a casual hook-up with the likes of Mike Daughtry is not something I'm equipped for.

"We promised to go slow." I sit up and turn toward him, covering my naked front with both hands.

"We are going slow." His skin is flushed, his gaze intensely focused on my breasts.

"I wasn't talking about foreplay."

"Neither was I. But I won't deny what's happening between us. Or stop it."

"I need more time."

"For what?"

"To figure this out."

He releases me and sits at the far side of the couch. "Why are you here, Zoe? Why did you come to Mexico with me?"

"Lots of reasons... I'm not sure anymore." It's strange but true.

"Lots?" We stare at each other before Mike throws a towel across my exposed breasts. "Do tell."

I wrap the towel around myself, collecting my bits along with my thoughts. "I've never been on a real vacation before. I wanted to see the ocean."

"So you're here for the views?"

"Partly," I admit. "But I didn't want to be alone for the holiday, either."

"Anything else?" He's openly irritated.

"I wanted to sort out my feelings about us."

"And how's that working for you?" He folds his arms.

"I could ask the same thing of you. The last time we were together, you were in a bad place yourself. Why me?" I ask. "Was I your first choice to come here with, or was there someone else?"

He says nothing, but the line of his mouth hardens.

"You can be overwhelming. And if you're the type of woman who likes being overwhelmed with exotic vacations, gourmet meals, and tropical adventures, you're very easy to like. Is that what you want?"

Mike starts to speak, but he's interrupted.

"Hello? Hello, in there? You ordered lunch in your canopy today?"

"Just a minute." Mike breaks eye contact with me,

leaping off the couch and placing his body between my topless form and the entrance to the canopy.

He talks to them outside for a moment while I pull my kaftan back over my head and smooth it down. I get up and put the aloe gel back into the cooler, then snap it shut loudly. When I turn around, two men with trays and a cooler enter our canopy and place the lunch on our small end tables.

As Mike confirms the order with the hotel staff, I think back to the first time we met at the hospital. He'd gotten into a fight over a woman and lost. It's not really fair, to either of us, that I know about that.

But I can't shake the fear I'm not his first choice of a travel companion and that makes me reluctant to explore my true feelings for him.

"Take this, Zoe." Mike sets a small tray down beside my feet on the couch. He does the same for the second tray, only he leaves it there and walks to the canopy entrance.

"Where are you going?" I ask.

"I'm not hungry. Think I'll head back out."

"Mike, don't be like this. Please."

"It's okay." His casual smile doesn't reach his eyes. "You're not the first girl who's gone to the dance with someone just because he had a ticket." He shrugs. "See you back at the villa."

Without another word, he scoops up his snorkel gear and trots back toward the water.

He's not the only one who doesn't feel like eating.

MIKE

"Wow." Zoe's eyes widen. "Is that real?"

"Yeah. Most of it anyway." Her excitement is proof I chose our next activity well. "The waterfall is natural, and so is the plunge pool at the base. But the secondary pools beneath it are manmade."

I watch her stop at the end of the jungle footpath and stare up at the one-hundred-fifty-foot waterfall. It's a beautiful place that never disappoints, no matter how many times I return. With any luck, it will drive me to a much-needed distraction from Zoe.

After she banned me from her strike zone, I snorkeled for another hour before enjoying a lunch of warm beer and cold beef tenderloin.

Alone.

I remind myself for the millionth time that I didn't bring Zoe here expecting her to hop right into bed. Maybe I hoped it a little more than I should have. Okay, a lot more.

But the fact is, we've already done that. And it was... Mindblowing. So much so that the whole point of this trip was to see if there was anything more to our attraction than just *that*.

She struggles with it, too. The way she checks me out, her physical responses. She's fighting it tooth-and-nail right along with me.

By the time I returned to the villa yesterday, Zoe had showered, dressed and was eager to go into town. We took a guided tour, then stumbled on a boat rental place and went for a two-hour ride along the coast.

It was late when we return to the hotel. We ate a quick supper before falling into separate beds, exhausted. The tense lack of satisfaction remained, but we were too worn out to give a fuck. Literally and otherwise.

If I'm fair, I should be grateful. If I'm honest, it makes me cranky.

"How long can we stay here?" Zoe asks.

"We have it to ourselves for the afternoon. It needs to be booked in advance. But we can leave anytime. Would you like to go horseback riding this evening on the beach at sunset? There's a place near here."

"I don't know how to ride a horse."

"That's okay. They're used to that. They'll find you one for beginners."

She sighs and starts toward the edge of the greenery surrounding the lower pools. "Can we decide later? It's nice here and we've been so busy."

"Sure, Zoe. But the longer we wait, the harder it will get." What the *hell* did I say? "We should call before five to make sure they have a horse you can ride."

For fuck's sake, stop talking, asshole.

"Please. This will be my first time, and I need one that's slow and gentle," she replies.

"I'll do my best." I bite the side of my cheek and stride past her to the large pool, where I toss my cooler and backpack on the ground and strip off my long-sleeved T-shirt.

"Mike, what are you doing?" Zoe asks.

I turn to find her checking me out from behind. Those full cherry-red lips are parted in an eager oval while her heated big black eyes brim with lust she tries to suppress by blinking.

It doesn't work.

Damn it, Zoe, don't look at me like that if all you're going to do is look.

The second best way to deal with unspent lust is the autocorrect feature of my right hand. But when what I want is so close but still so far away, that option can make things feel even shittier, so I've abstained from that, too.

For now

"Getting wet. I need to cool off." Without another word. I hop into the pool and wade toward the waterfall.

The water's cooler than the air, but it's still warm. The entire resort is built on the jungle's edge, but in this hot steamy summer season, the surface water feels like a bath you'd welcome during a harsh Chicago winter because the stream feeding the waterfall is exposed to brutal direct sunlight along its winding path.

Fortunately, the water cools about three feet under the surface. The forest canopy protects the falls from the sun, which is why I chose this venue. I wanted to protect Zoe from sunburn and myself from her lying around the villa half dressed for the day. That I can't take right now.

"Is it safe?" she calls from the shore.

"Safe? Of course, it's safe. Come on."

Zoe dips a tentative toe in the pool and wriggles it around. She's wearing the tiniest pink polka-dot string bikini bottom with a gray cropped T-shirt. She's been slathering herself in sunscreen the entire trip, but her skin is a persistent lobster red.

A tinge of guilt shudders through me. With her super dark hair and eyes, it didn't occur to me that Zoe would burn so badly. Hell, I'm a blue-eyed blond and I'm doing better than she is right now.

"Zoe, get in the water." I insist. "Try to avoid the sun when you can."

Zoe nods, takes a few steps back, then hurls herself into the pool. When the huge splash she created subsides, she looks around, shocked.

"You still alive?" I ask.

"Yeah." She dog paddles over. "Can we check out the waterfall?"

"Sure. It's a plunge waterfall. The water stream loses contact with the rock, so there's actually a little alcove just behind it you can stand under."

"How do you know?"

Because I've been here before. The owners had shown me before I became a shareholder. And whenever I need peace and clarity, this is one of my favorite spots on planet earth. I want to tell her all these things, but I can't right now. Damn, I'm sick of lying to her.

Is that why I invited her here?

"Let's check it out." I avoid her question.

She frowns at my response, but it passes quickly as she hurries toward the falls.

I wade out of the pool alongside the narrow path that leads behind the waterfall and wait for her.

"Come on." I stretch my hand out to her, and she grabs it to steady herself on the path. "This'll be cool."

"Wait!" She reaches up to my shoulder and pulls back gently. "Are there any bats in there?"

"Bats? You really are a city girl, aren't you?"

"Are there?" she persists.

"I don't think so. But I'll go first if it makes you feel better."

"Thanks." She nods and grabs my hand, letting me lead her behind the waterfall curtain. The water separates from the rock wall thirty feet in the air while the earth we're standing on feels like a mixture of clay and fine sand.

Zoe lets go of me and places a tentative hand into the stream of rushing water. She giggles, then splashes me. As she runs in and out of the falls like an excited child, I move inch by inch into the falls and let the water roll over me. I close my eyes as the cascading motion drowns out my thoughts and surrounding reality for a few moments.

But it doesn't last.

"Mike? Mike." She pulls me out of the waterfall. "Listen."

I step into the alcove and Zoe pretends to laugh. As the sound of her laughter echoes off the sheer rock walls, there's an answer. A rapid click-click-click, followed by a musical sound, and then more clicks.

Then the strangest thing happens. The musical sound keeps time with the beat of the clicks.

"Is that…birds?" I wonder aloud.

"No. Bats." She scours the inside of the alcove with sharp eyes. "There!" she rasps and points to a group of brownish gray spots that move in a wavelike motion along the bottom ridge. "I'm done." Zoe leaps through the waterfall and into the pool.

I watch her leave through the sheer fine mist, her motion a combination of running and swimming, as if the hounds of hell were at her heels. It's a bit comical, actually. Bats have no interest in humans and most eat fruit or mosquitos.

My eyes dart up to the jagged rock ceiling of the alcove, which appears to be moving. After a few more clicks, the excitement in the air subsides and the motion stills. I follow her out through the waterfall. She's almost to the edge of the first pond before I catch up to her.

"Take it easy," I tell her, before falling down in the water next to her and laughing.

"You *lied!*" She sounds unhinged. "Damn it, I hate bats!"

"They're usually harmless and don't bother humans."

"Says he who's never been treated for rabies."

"What?"

I study Zoe as she huddles under the clear waters

against the stone wall of the manmade pond. Her body shivers, despite the intense jungle heat.

"Take it easy, hon." I huddle against her under the water. "It's okay. You're safe now."

It's a few minutes before her breathing normalizes and she stops shaking. After that, she speaks quickly and quietly.

"One time, when I was a kid during a nasty winter, it was too cold to go outside." She rocks herself back and forth. "Our house is small, and I was bored at home with nothing to do. So I went up to our dreary little attic and tried to clear out a space to play. That's when I found them."

"Found what? Bats? In your house?"

"Yeah."

"That's freaky."

"There was a crack in the plaster between the chimney and the wall. At least that's what the pest removal guy told my mother." She burrows under my arm and looks back at the waterfall. "I'd dragged some boxes over by the crack and shoved them hard against it. That's when the angry clicking started. I didn't know what it was until a bat found its way out between the boxes and bit me on the arm."

Zoe shuts her eyes hard at the memory. Tense lines appear at their corners, along with a large 'W' that furls between her eyebrows. Instinctively, I draw her body into mine then wrap my legs along the sides of hers. As I curl my arms around her shoulders, she presses her back against my chest.

"They tested all the bats, but since they could enter

and leave through the hole in the plaster, no one was ever certain they found the one that bit me. I was treated for rabies as a precaution. Five painful injections over a month."

"I'm so sorry I laughed, Zoe." Her story makes me shudder with guilt. "I didn't know what happened to you." I grip her shoulders protectively. "And I didn't know there would be bats here."

"It's not your fault." She sighs and rests the back of her head against my collarbone. "How could you know about something like that?"

She doesn't expect me to answer, but her question fills me with guilt, which makes me want to distract us both. With her body pressed against me, and that wet T-shirt that leaves nothing to the imagination, well, distraction comes easy.

My lips descend onto hers, and I kiss Zoe with all the restless frustration pent up inside me, consequences be damned. Only instead of receiving a slap in the face or elbow to the groin, something unexpected happens.

She kisses me back. Like she wants it. Like she means it.

"Zoe…"

She responds with a groan and shifts her body around to straddle me. With a knee on each side of my thighs, she pins me to the wall. It would be easy to escape since she's so much smaller than me. But the gentle strokes of her hand across my body, along with her insistent kisses are a much more potent force. I couldn't be more subdued if boulders were piled on top of me.

I groan as her lips leave mine and descend the plains of my chest until they reach the waterline of the pool. Her tongue dips into the water, then dances around the edges of my navel, before skating back up to the base of my throat.

Zoe's see-through T-shirt clings to her curves, and the view from here evokes a strong rush of heat. I struggle to pull the clingy fabric from her body, but it sticks to her skin, refusing to cooperate. Impatience overcomes me, and I rip the thin, filmy fabric of the shirt up her back.

She gasps at the sound and looks up at me. I meet her eyes, daring her to protest. She doesn't. Instead, she holds my gaze while she strips the ripped shirt off her shoulders and slides it away before tossing the tattered cloth behind me.

I rest my forehead against her chest while I lick and kiss the cleft between her breasts. My fingers tease her tender nipples, and she responds with a fierce moan as she arches her hips into mine.

"God damn it, Zoe. Don't fuck with me. If you're going to call time, do it. Right now."

ZOE

I hold Mike's gaze, while my hands dive under the water and rest on the waist of his board shorts. "Take these off," I insist.

"You do it," Mike dares me.

It's no use. I'm way too attracted to him. And my resolve isn't helped by the fact that I know from our time at St. Rafe's that he's an energetic, passionate lover. Even though I can't shake the feeling he's not being entirely truthful about... *something,* our chemistry is the real deal.

Besides, not all our shit is for sharing. Maybe Mike's got scars he doesn't want me, or anyone else, to see. That doesn't make him a bad person.

I search for snaps to unbutton and drawstrings to untie. I struggle to pull his shorts off, but his bulging front prevents me.

"Careful, Zoe." Mike lifts me off, then slides his shorts down and over his bulging erection. As he stands,

I keep hold of his waistband, pulling the wet fabric down over his muscular thighs.

There's a moment of humorous hesitation as our eyes meet. I'm on my knees and he's staring down at me over his bulging erection with a priceless expression on his face. It gives me the distinct feeling he's enjoying the view and committing it to memory.

Once he's done, he pulls me from the water and tosses me over his shoulder.

"What are you doing?"

"Taking this someplace where we can work it." Mike scopes out the area around the waterfall, then steps out of his shorts without breaking stride. I'm mesmerized by the view of his perfect backside and powerful legs as he moves along as though I'm weightless.

Mike drops to his knees, and a moment later I'm flat on my back, my skin scraping against the springy, spongy moss that makes up the canopy of the forest floor.

Our fingers get tangled in a breathless struggle to peel my bikini bottoms from the wet flesh of my hips and thighs. When they're finally off, a flash of feral still-ness hangs in the air. There are no words, just eye contact and pure heat—a final check before we cross the point of no return together.

Even if I wanted to I couldn't refuse.

Mike's taut gold skin glistens in the sunshine, almost the same color as his hair. He kneels before me, breathing heavily, naked and muscular. His arms are stretched apart, hovering near my legs. His deep blue eyes dart back and forth between my face and breasts, which rise and fall with my rapid breathing.

He's waiting. For me.

It doesn't take long. I prop myself up on one elbow and reach for him with the opposite hand. Mike collapses between my thighs and brings his face down to mine. He gives me a pleased, knowing smile, before his lips descend on mine with gentlest of kisses. I return the kiss while arching into him.

"We're good, right? Christ, please say yes."

"We're good. Now come here."

Without another word, he enters me with a swift, solid stroke. I draw a sharp breath at his suddenness, and Mike stills a moment before his whole body shudders. My knees rise up along his body and he grips them in his strong hands, splitting me wider as he burrows even deeper.

"Ahh," I cry out, grinding in unison with him, letting him take me wherever he wants to go.

"We've got all day." He grips the sides of my hips, slowing down my thrusts. "Let's take our time."

"Is this okay?" I grind out a slower rhythm.

"Perfect." He shudders. "No one's getting left behind. I'll be here when you're ready."

With a mixture of exquisite passion and disciplined patience, he controls the speed and rhythm of our irre-sistible tempo. When I move too quickly, he slows his strokes to a near stop. His mouth softens, brushing my nape and temples, coaxing me to slow down and revel in his tenderness.

When he needs... more for himself the pace of his

thrusts become stronger and deeper. Those tender kisses turn to tiny bites at the base of my throat, and he twists the tips of my breasts, sending raw sensation throughout my body, urging the motion of my hips against him.

"Oh, god," I groan as Mike takes me through several mind-blowing rounds of our urgent, pulsing journey. But on this final crest, our joined bodies move in perfect unison, igniting a single, sublime, never-ending moment.

Damn, he's *good* at this.

I force myself to ignore the hows and whos of Mike's mad skills and surrender myself to oblivion.

MIKE

"GOD *DAMN,* ZOE." I HISS OUT THE WORDS JUST BEFORE
I start to come.

She's straddled on top, grinding me inside her with
that reckless, unrestrained energy of hers. My stubble
scrapes the tender flesh of her breasts as they rub against
me. The last thing I remember is tasting the sting of
sweat and blood as I bury my face between them,
powerless.

Seconds later, a high-pitched grunt fills the air. Zoe's
gyrations become irregular and I feel her inner core
shudder around my now-satiated erection. I wait as long
as I can, but when her ferocious internal quivering
ceases, I fall back onto a pile of pillows and unwashed
sheets covering the king-sized bed in the master
bedroom of my villa.

Unjoined, she follows me down, resting her head in
the crook of my arm while she presses the front of her

body against mine. I feel the rapid beating of her heart, in perfect sync with the silent rushing sound in my ears. From the moment Zoe committed to sex, she put her whole heart and soul into it, making it impossible for me to give any less.

"Hey, you," she says after her breathing slows down.

"Hey, you back." I slide a hand down and gently grip her ass.

"You okay?" she asks.

"Wrecked. You?"

"Same here." She props herself up and gives me a playful kiss on the lips. "Thank you."

"Damn, Zo-Zo. Look at you." I trace a gentle finger over the scratches on her breast and chest. "Fuck! I'm so sorry."

"Wow." She pokes at them herself. "They look worse than they feel." She rubs the sides of my face. "You are starting to resemble a porcupine, though."

"Well, if you'd let me out of bed long enough to shave…"

"I wasn't complaining." She kisses the tip of my nose. "And like I said, it looks worse than it is."

I kiss her forehead and gaze out the open French doors that overlook the ocean. There's still plenty of sunlight, but judging from the receding haze over the water, it's late afternoon. Our trip to the waterfall was two days ago, and since then we've spent most of our time horizontal in my villa.

"Tonight's our last night," I remind her.

"I know." She sighs. "I can't believe it's almost time

to leave." She sits up next to me. "I've had a wonderful mind-blowing time. With *you*. Thank you."

"You're welcome." I kiss the top of her head. "Let's eat in the hotel seaside restaurant tonight. We'll get cleaned up, wear actual clothes—"

"– something we haven't done in a few days."

"Exactly. It will also give the staff a chance to get in here."

Uncollected room service trays litter the villa. We're out of clean towels, and the sheets on *all* the beds need to be changed. What a fucking disaster zone.

"Why are you smiling?" she asks.

"No reason. Just happy." I drag my naked body out of bed and survey the room for clothes. The last time I'd worn any was the living room. "I'll collect the trays, call room service and ask them to bring up some towels. Then I'll get a reservation for tonight."

"Do I have time for a swim?"

"Probably not right now. Besides, I'd rather you clean up those scratches and put antibiotic cream on them. Nurse Zoe."

"Probably a good idea." She checks her breasts out, then groans before rolling off the bedside and landing on her feet. "And maybe you should consider a shave." She stretches up on her toes and kisses my rough cheek.

"On it," I promise.

~

"You look good in clothes. Who knew?" I let her catch me checking out her ass as I pull the chair out. She's wearing this tight, hot pink cap sleeve dress with a frilly ruffle at the waist. And if I'm not mistaken, a lacy red thong underneath.

"Thank you." She smiles over her shoulder at me before sitting. "Nice shave."

"You'll be thanking me for that again later," I whisper in her ear when she settles into the chair.

"Here's hoping."

"You bring that dress from Chicago?" I ask, sitting next to her. "It's a keeper."

"And the compliments keep on coming."

"I'm in a good mood and it's been a great trip."

"It really has. To think I'll be back at work the day after tomorrow…"

"Fuck. Don't think about that." My own problems with Janet and the company come rushing back to me. But being here with Zoe makes it easier to forget the whole mess. "I know it doesn't seem like it, but Chicago's a world away. Let's enjoy the distance while we can."

"Agreed. I'd drink to it if I could."

"You want to do a few shots of tequila before dinner?"

"I bet it's superb here."

"Some of the best anywhere," I promise.

"Well, set me up then."

We enjoy a few rounds of Tres-Quatro-Cinco, but before we order dinner, Zoe looks down at her cleavage and notices a band-aid popping out of the top of her dress.

"Oh, damn." She covers her breast. "I need to fix this. Where are the bathrooms?"

"Back past the entrance." I stand to get her chair, but she stops me.

"Back soon," she tells me before leaving the restaurant.

ZOE

Maybe it's the architecture, the way the building and nature seem to merge flawlessly into the structure of the hotel. Maybe it's the indigenous art, displayed in every room and corridor. Or perhaps I'm just lost in happy thoughts of Mike and me together.

Whatever the reason, I can't find the bathroom. Hell, after wandering distracted for a good five minutes, I don't even know how to get back to the restaurant. Amusement becomes annoyance when I find myself at hotel front desk, looking around like the lost tourist I am.

"Good evening, Ms. Inglot," an attractive, middle-aged Latino man calls from behind a large desk in the lobby.

"I'm sorry, have we met?" I approach.

"We have, on the day you arrived." He stands. "You're staying in Mr. Daughtry's villa. Yes?"

Mr. Daughtry's villa. There's something about the way he says it that strikes me as odd. "Yes, that's right."

"I'm Hector Avila, one of the hotel managers." He extends his hand. "I hope you're enjoying your stay here."

"Absolutely. Everything has been wonderful. The food. The on-site facilities. And the people working here are all so kind and helpful."

"We try very hard to take excellent care of all our guests, especially our owners and partners," he explains.

I nod sagely for a moment before speaking. "Owners and partners? I don't understand."

"Like many luxury properties, we offer both ownership and rental opportunities."

"I see." I take a wild stab in the dark. "So there are other privately owned villas on the property as well? Like Mr. Daughtry's?"

"Yes. Twelve in all. The entire development was new when Mr. Daughtry made his purchase. At the time, he had his pick of the villas. But we've recently sold the last one."

Mother*fucker*.

"Well… congratulations." A shock wave surges through my body. "Can you please tell me the way to the restaurant, Mr. Avila?"

"I'll walk you out to the main hall." He leads me across the exotic, eco-friendly lobby. He's pointing out the corridor while he gives me directions, but my mind is elsewhere.

I'm preoccupied with the fact that Mike lied, and that he owns the two-bedroom oceanfront palace we've been holed up in all week. What really hurts is that he *knew* I didn't want to be with someone like him. Someone who lied so easily, presumed so casually, deceived so readily to get his way.

And why me? Judging from the star treatment I'd received in his bed all week, there's no shortage of female takers for what he's offering. Mike is the total package without his obvious wealth.

Kind. Funny. Smart. Gorgeous. Great in the sack.

An ember of sympathy for my mother engulfs me. She never disses my father, but she never talks about him, either. I realize now how hard it must have been for her to choose between giving up and giving in, especially if she liked him half as much as I like Mike.

But I'm not my mother. I've seen what happens when you try to ignore deceit in a relationship. It's not something I can do. Or something I can live with.

"… and if you need anything else while you're here, please contact me." He hands me his card.

I glance at it quickly. Underneath the name of the hotel, in small italicized print there's a single phrase. *A joint venture of Punta de Mita ECO Resorts and DC-squared.*

DC-squared? I've seen that before, but I can't remember where. Besides, I'm in too much shock to process anymore. I tuck his card inside the front flap of my tiny purse.

"Thank you, Mr. Avila. You've been very helpful."

MIKE

"You'll never guess what happened, Zoe," Mike
tells me after returning from the airline check-in counter.

"What? Don't tell me they've bumped us." She
sounds horrified.

"Actually, we've been upgraded. To first class."

"Really?" Zoe eyes me suspiciously. "How did that
happen?"

"Frequent flyer points." I shrug. "Had more than I
thought."

"Enough for two first-class tickets from Puerto
Vallarta to Chicago? You must. Travel. A lot." She tilts
her head. "Where do you go?"

"All over." I'm easing into being truthful with her.
"Let's get the bags and head over to the VIP lounge so
we can relax before the flight." I glance at my watch.
"We've got about an hour."

"Mike." She stops me from picking up her carry-on
case.

"What?"

"Where do you go when you travel?"

"Damn, you're feisty today." She's been acting weird since dinner yesterday. "I travel all over for MMA fights. Can I take the bag now?"

"I've got it," she replies.

"Well, suit yourself. The first-class lounge is this way… You coming?"

She looks like she's about to say no, but then she suddenly grabs her bag and stands. "Sure. Let's go."

Fuck. It doesn't take a genius to see that she's upset about something.

Last night, Zoe barely touched her dinner, and when we returned to the villa, she'd wanted to go for a swim. Alone.

"Um, okay," I'd told her, before taking a shower and heading to bed to wait for her.

She stumbled in after midnight, wearing granny sweats and a baggy tee-shirt. She eased herself down onto the king-sized bed, then crawled to the corner farthest away from my naked body.

At that point, I'd thought she was a little over-sexed, maybe even a little sore, and she didn't want to tell me or say no if I asked for it. It was hard to blame her for that after the last few days, so I'd said I was tired, then kissed her goodnight and rolled away. A few minutes later, she slid out of bed and left for the night.

She's been in the same happy place all damn day.

"I need a minute here, Zoe." At the entrance of the first-class lounge, I show the attendant our tickets and my VIP card. He slides it into the reader, looks up at his screen and smiles.

"Welcome back, Mr. Daughtry. Please enjoy the amenities."

He looks over at Zoe and nods.

"Thank you." When I turn around to look at Zoe, she's giving me a death glare. "What?" I ask, unable to hide my impatience.

"'Welcome back, Mr. Daughtry?'" she repeats. "You told me you won this trip in a sales contest at work."

Oh *shit.*

"Let's discuss this inside." I usher her through the double glass doors to the lounge area. Thankfully, two overstuffed chairs in a quiet corner are vacant. "These good?" I ask.

"Fine with me," she replies, tossing her bag on the ground next to them. I wait for her to choose a chair before I settle in next to her. "When were you here last? And why?"

Be careful, I warn myself.

"Zoe, I never said I hadn't been here before." A cold sweat breaks out at the nape of my neck. "The company I work for has a business relationship with the resort."

"So you were here on business?" I ask.

"No." I cross my legs and fold my hands over my knee. "When the property isn't being used for business, it's sometimes available."

"Available? For what?" Her question is filled with hostile disbelief.

She knows something's up. It was only a matter of time. And truthfully, the stress of keeping track of everything I tell her is getting to me. But given Zoe's history with her ex, I want to do this in stages. Being who and what I am doesn't make me a bad guy—there's just less of an incentive to be good.

"For whatever… January was the last time I was here. I came to watch the baby humpback whales."

"You did what?"

"This place is famous for whale watching. January is when the babies are born." My eyes hold hers. "I come here to enjoy…nature, wildlife, the outdoors. All the things I missed out on growing up a city kid."

She looks away, her expression conflicted. I'm telling her the truth, but she lacks the context to know that. Since I'm on thin ice with her, she's not likely to give me the benefit of any doubt.

"Did you come here…with that woman? The one you got into a fight over the day we met in the ER?"

My head snaps back at her question. "No. Never. I've never brought someone I'm seeing here before."

"So why me?"

"I wanted to get away, and I wanted to be with you. The rest I'm still trying to figure out." I reach out and cover her hand with mine. "And I'm trying to give you time to do the same."

Her body stills when I touch her. Moments pass, then she shifts, taking her hand away.

"What do you want from me, Zoe? Would you rather I lie about my feelings?"

"I'd rather you not lie at all," she snaps.

"Lie to you? About what?"

Zoe draws her knees into chest, resting her feet on

the edge of the chair. "I don't believe you won this trip in any damn contest. And I don't believe we just lucked into two first-class airline tickets."

"Okay. Maybe not." I let the truth start to emerge. "So what?"

"So what?" her eyes widen in disbelief. "So maybe I don't like being lied to, that's what."

"Zoe… Could you afford to stay in a luxury resort? Or buy first-class airline tickets?"

She glares at me. "You *know* I can't."

"Exactly. I didn't want you to say no because you were freaking about the cost, and I sure as hell didn't want to spend my vacation in a Motel Six that was driving distance from some nameless midwestern lake." I shift away from her. "What I told you solved everyone's problems."

"Yours maybe. Not mine." Zoe rises from her chair and grabs her carry-on bag. "I don't like lies. Or being manipulated. Or misled into making a choice I wouldn't have normally made."

"You wouldn't have gone on vacation with me?" I ask.

"I would've gone on vacation with you. But not here."

"Because of the money?" I don't believe this.

"Exactly," she replies.

"Right. Don't you see? That's why I lied."

"Okay, I'm done now."

"Where are you going?" I ask.

"To the restroom. Then I'll to go eat before this

flight." Her eyes meet mine. "Give me my ticket, please."

"Zoe..."

"Look, we've got a long flight ahead of us. Until then, let's keep our distance, okay?"

"Fine." I reach into the outside pocket of my carry-on and pull out two tickets. I hand her one, and she snatches it from my hand.

"Thanks," she tells me, before walking away.

Damn, it's going to be a long plane ride home...

~

W hat a ride from hell. And I don't mean the mile high club.

I didn't see Zoe until it was time to board, and she had waited until the last possible moment. When she arrived at the seat next to me, she'd barely said hello, then had put on her headphones and went to sleep. Or at least pretended. She fucking ignored me the whole flight, but I suppose it was better than getting into a major blowout on the plane.

She'd collected her suitcase from baggage claim before me and headed into customs, where I almost caught up with her. Now she's racing to the airport shuttle counter like hell in heels. It's Sunday afternoon following a major holiday, and the terminal is crowded and hectic. Keeping track of her through the crowd is getting tough.

"Zoe, wait," I call to out her from a few steps behind.

"Let me at least take you home. I have a car service waiting."

"I'll take the shuttle. Thanks." She keeps moving while she talks.

I squeeze past the person between us and touch her arm. "Don't be like this. It's not right."

"Not right? You've got to be kidding me."

I steer her toward the glass wall alongside the automatic doors. It's a dead space, though it's far from private. But it's out of the path of people moving through the airport, while the din of activity and many voices provides some white noise for our conversation.

When we arrive, I park my rolling suitcase in front of her path out and lean on it.

"Okay Zoe, I lied to you about the winning the trip. But while it might be hard for you to believe, women find me attractive *before* they get a clue about my financial status. I try to steer clear of the topic as long as I can. And yes, I've lied to avoid it."

"There it is again." She gives me a disgusted shake of her head.

"There is what again?" I fold my arms..

"That self-indulgent sense of entitlement masquerading as expediency. I don't want any part of it. And you knew that. I told you the day you showed up at my work. After, after..." Her voice trails off.

I lean my elbow onto the glass wall next to her before rubbing my temples.

"You're bitching out the wrong guy, Zoe. Your ex is a real piece of work. And I've told you before, Paul's not rich. He's a doctor. That's not bad, but it's not rich." I shake my head and shrug.

"To quote an old movie, 'just how many yachts can you water-ski behind?'"

Here we go again. The context problem. She doesn't trust me enough to believe what I'm telling her. And she doesn't know enough to judge for herself.

"My dad told me something a long time ago." I take a breath, then exhale slowly. "He said, 'Mike, the first million is tough. Really tough. After that, things get easy.'"

"What's that supposed to mean?"

"When you're on your way to making that first million, it's all about making that pile bigger and bigger. Some people get a little obsessive about it. And stingy. That stinginess can spill over into other areas of their lives." My other hand strokes her cheek. "Sound familiar?"

She closes her eyes, hard. "Maybe."

"I'm not like that, Zoe. And I didn't want you writing me off because someone else treated you badly."

Her shoulders fall. "You're right about that. It wasn't fair to pre-judge you because of someone else's behavior."

"No, it wasn't." I exhale.

"I like you, Zoe. I think you like me. We had a really great time together. It means a lot to me that…what happened, happened with you thinking that the trip was only a prize." I place a gentle kiss on top of her forehead.

"I like you too. I think." She throws that last part in

before rubbing my hand resting on her cheek. "But no more lies. Especially if it's to manipulate me into making a decision. No matter how well-intentioned."

"I was just trying to—"

"Mike!"

"Okay. Promise."

"And one more thing. We need to slow down."

"Slow down? What does that mean?"

She sighs. "There are probably things about me that are going to surprise you, too. Let's just deal with them as they come, okay? I don't want to feel like I've got to rush to tell you stuff."

"Same here. That's why I lied about the trip."

Zoe frowns at me, but before she can speak, I cut her off.

"Look, I'm sorry, okay?" I blurt out. "I'm used to getting the check. It's no big deal. Really. If we were still together in six months, I'd have expected you to figure it out. And if you bothered to ask, to be amused by my answer. I never anticipated you'd feel deceived. Or get this pissed off."

"Well, I did."

"I don't know what else to say." It's the truth. "I'm sorry. Can we go home now? Please?"

Her frown transforms into a tired smile. "Yes, please."

ZOE

"Mike, it's fine," I tell him as he slides out of the car after me.

"Relax and let me help you with your bag. Christ, it's bigger than you are." Mike hands the driver a twenty-dollar bill. "Give me a few minutes,"

The driver sets my suitcase down on the sidewalk and nods at Mike before taking the money.

Shit. It's about five o'clock on a Sunday afternoon. Chloe and Mom are probably both here. I don't want to do the meet the family thing. But Mike's been here twice now, and it does feel rude to not let him in the house.

Reluctantly, I lead the way up to the front door. The plastic wheels make a clickety-clack sound as they catch on the cracks of the concrete pavement. Mike comes to a stop just behind me. I fumble for my key, but before it finds its way into the lock, the front door bursts open.

"Zoe!" Chloe says. "Happy fourth. I missed you."

"Happy Fourth." I give her a hug. "I missed you, too."

I feel Chloe stiffen against me. "Hi," she says to Mike over my shoulder. "Who are you?"

I clear my throat and take a step back. "Chloe, this is Mike. Mike, this is my little sister."

"Hey, Chloe." Mike smiles and nods at her.

I hadn't told Chloe much about my plans. Only that I wouldn't be around for the holiday and that I'd be back today. But it doesn't take long for my sweet, savvy streetwise sister to put things together.

"Hi-i." She glances down at my suitcase, up at him, and over to me. "Would you like to come in?"

"Sure." He responds, holding the door open as he wheels my suitcase in behind me.

Mike hesitates a moment as he looks around. Our house is small, and you can see everything from the door. The living room overlooks the street, the entry to the kitchen behind it. To the right of the front door is a narrow hallway that leads to our bedrooms in the back of the house.

"Where should I put your suitcase?" he asks.

"You can just leave it there. I'll take it later."

"Would like something, Mike?" Chloe asks. "Water? I think we still have coffee. Or a Red Bull?"

"Just water, if you don't mind."

"I'll get it," I tell Chloe. As I move past her into the kitchen, I whisper, "Is Mom home?"

"She's asleep."

I nod. Thank heaven for tender mercies.

As I clank through the kitchen to get a water glass,

Chloe and Mike's happy chatter echoes off the plaster walls of our living room. His easygoing charm and her vivacious personality make me smile. They exchange the most trivial of small-talk and manage to sound politely fascinated with each other. They both have that gift of easy likability.

Their personalities mesh well.

As I fill the glass from a jug in our refrigerator, I hear noise coming from my mother's room next to the kitchen. Even though she sleeps a lot during the day, she's always been particular about not coming out in her pajamas if we've got company. Most of the time, she sleeps through and it's okay because people know about her schedule.

Quick familiar footsteps and the creaky sound of her closet door tell me she intends to make an appearance. I rush into the living room, hoping to get Mike out of the house before she emerges. That would be too much for one day.

"Here you go, Mike." Dread washes over me as I note that he's taken a seat on our weathered Lazy Boy chair, next to the couch facing Chloe. They both look settled with no plans to leave. He takes the glass and waits for me to sit before he drinks.

I don't.

Mike gives me a killer smile, clears his throat, and looks back at Chloe. "Your sister was just telling me all about her plans for school." Then he brings his lips to the glass and takes a long, slow gulp.

Damn it. "Don't you have to go? Doesn't the car have to leave?"

Mike shrugs. "He'll call me when we need to go."

Behind me, I hear my mother's door open and her rapid footsteps approaching.

This is going to happen.

I stare out the living room window and take a deep breath before looking toward Mike. He's watching me intently, and I meet his gaze with a look of dread.

"Hello," my mother announces as she enters the living room. "I thought I heard you, Zoe. How was your trip?"

"It was fine, Mom. I had a great time."

Behind me, the Lazy Boy chair creaks as Mike gets to his feet. He steps behind me and puts his hand on my shoulder. "Hi. You must be Zoe's mom."

"Yes." Mom tucks a strand of silver-blonde hair behind her ear. "Audrea Inglot." She nods at him.

"I'm Mike," He extends his hand. "It's nice to meet you Ms.—"

"Audrea, please."

"Audrea." I watch as Mike flashes her that lethal smile as he takes her hand. Yeah, those Mike Daughtry dimples are working their magic on my mom.

But my mom's got her own special brand of mojo.

"So, how do you two know each other?" Mom's gaze shifts back and forth between us.

"We met at a party." Mike speaks before I do.

"A party?" Mom sounds surprised. "Zoe doesn't go to many parties."

Thanks, Mom.

"Well, we actually met in the ER before. It kind of

broke the ice when we ran into each other again," Mike replies.

"The ER? What happened?" Mom asks.

"I got punched in the eye."

"Punched in the eye?" Mom repeats. "How awful."

"No worries." Mike tries to calm her. "It was a sparring accident."

"A what?" she repeats.

"Mike's an MMA fighter, Mom." I wrap my arm around Mike's waist and smile at her. "He got hurt while he was training."

"A fighter?" Her mouth forms an oval, and her gaze shifts back and forth between us. "Is that…a job? Or a hobby?" she asks after an awkward silence.

Oh, here it comes.

"It's both, I guess." Mike's tone is easy going.

"Mmm… Does that pay well?"

Welcome to hell.

"It can for some guys," Mike answers.

"Oh. Are you one of those guys?" she asks.

Mike stiffens against my arm.

Shoot me now.

"Mom, Mike has an airport taxi waiting for him outside." I lean against Mike's hip and his weight shifts. "He should go."

"Of course," my mother agrees. "I didn't mean to keep you."

"It was nice meeting you, Audrea." Mike smiles. "I'm sure we'll see each other again."

"I hope so, too," Chloe calls from the couch when Mom remains silent an instant too long.

Mike walks toward the door and stops. "Good luck with school, Chloe."

"Thanks." Chloe smiles.

"I'll walk out with you," I announce to everyone.

"Thank you." Mike opens the front door and I walk outside with him following behind me.

"Well," Mike says, closing the front door behind him. "That was…"

"Intrusive?" I wrap my arms around my torso and sigh. "I'm sorry. I warned you there were things about me that you were going to find odd and surprising. That's one of them."

Mike puts his arm around my shoulders as we dawdle down the concrete path to the street. "I'm not used to someone so probing about money. Especially the first time they meet."

"I know. But you have to understand, for people like us, money solves ninety percent of our day-to-day worries. That's why it's such a big deal." My arm circles his waist. "That was pretty out there, though."

"And what about you, Zoe? You're not immune to the convenience money buys? Or the peace of mind?"

"I have a plan. And it's working. Right now, that's where my peace of mind comes from."

"That's my girl." He plants a kiss on my forehead. "Don't worry about what happened with your mom. We'll compare notes after you've met my family."

Mike stops at the car door. We're silent for a few moments when he turns and locks me in a tight embrace. His lips find mine, and we share a deep, satisfying kiss.

Out in broad daylight, in front of my house, late on a Sunday afternoon.

"I had an amazing time." He gazes into my eyes.

"So did I. Thank you."

"You are… most welcome." He gives me a killer smile, then releases me to open the door. "Goodbye, Zoe," he tells me before closing the door.

"Bye," I reply.

As the car speeds off, I wonder if this is the last time we'll see each other.

Before leaving, Mike had done nothing more than thank me for a very nice trip. He was careful not make any future plans. No doubt he had presumed it would be easier from him to blend into my world than it would be for me to adjust to his.

After all, I'm not the one who lied about myself.

It still bothers me, the way he does that so easily. I know he considers it a convenience, and a way to spare others' feelings. It probably goes hand-in-hand with that instant likeability and that easy going, sexy-as-hell vibe he's got going on. Put it in that oh-so-hot package, and it works like a charm.

I know it does. Because despite understanding this, I still like him. A lot.

MIKE

DAMN.

I sigh in exasperation, then bring my Range Rover to a full stop on the main road before turning down the sharp, narrow driveway to my parents' home. Normally we meet at their townhouse in the city, but my mother prefers to spend summers at their lakefront home when they're around.

My SUV rolls to a stop next to the keypad near the security gate. Before I can punch in the code, the retractable doors slide to the edges of the asphalt pathway. That's probably my mom. She knew when I'd be here and likely used the cameras on top of the gate to watch for me.

After all, I've been summoned.

Without any pretense, I pull my car up the circular driveway and park next to the front entrance. I have no desire to be here, and as soon as this is over, I'm leaving again.

"Hello?" I close the front door loudly as I step in. "Mom? Dad?"

"Michael?" My mother's voice sounds far away as it echoes off the solid walls. "I thought you'd come through the side entrance," she says when she arrives.

"I can't stay long." I bend down to give her a hug and kiss on the cheek. "I need to get back to the city."

"We missed you on the fourth," my mother chides gently.

"I had business in Mexico."

Her perfectly shaped eyebrow arches. "Michael…"

"What? You know I've leveraged part of my trust fund assets to finance the ownership stake. Some things require personal attention. You of all people know that."

"Did you go alone?" she asks.

I meet her eyes without flinching. "Like I said… It was business."

"Then you should have rescheduled it and come for the holiday."

"Getting double-teamed by Dad and Janet for a royal ass chewing is not my idea of a holiday." I take a deep breath. "Stop pretending that all I missed out on were steaks and a yacht race."

"I wouldn't have let that happen," she insists.

"You wouldn't have been able to stop it. Dad, maybe, would have listened. But once Janet's on a rant, forget about it. I spared us all that. You should be thanking me instead of going for the guilt trip."

She gives me a sad expression before shaking her head.

"Where's Dad? Is Janet here, too?"

"He's in his study. And no, Janet's not here."

The study isn't a good sign. It would've been better if he were on the balcony or relaxing in the living room. Or hell, if he'd even come out to greet me when I arrived. Then I'd know he was glad to see me.

"No Janet? At least that's something. Are you coming?" I ask.

Mom shakes her head. "No."

"Well then, let's move this along so I can get the hell out of here." Without another word, I leave my mother standing alone in the foyer.

The hallway to the study is covered with silk wallpaper. The background is pale gold, and it has delicate trees with detailed leaves and beautiful red berries. As I walk down the hall, a variety of hand-painted partridges lead the way to the oak-paneled door of my father's office.

I've never liked this house. It doesn't make sense, but it's true. There were times I'd even boarded in high school rather than live here. It made my mother unhappy.

I rap my knuckles lightly on the closed door of my father's study.

"Come in."

When the door opens, my father's back is turned toward me. He's leaning against the frame of the open French doors that overlook Lake Michigan.

"Happy fourth, Mike."

"Thanks. You too." I step inside and close the door.

"How was Mexico?" he asks.

"Good. How was the yacht race?"

"Good." He turns to face me. "Our team won."

"Excellent." I take a seat in the large leather sectional next to the fireplace. "Looks like everyone had a good time."

"Not everyone." My father approaches the fireplace and sits across from me in the worn leather chair reserved exclusively for him.

"You mean Janet was unhappy?" My voice drips with cynicism. "That's a first."

"Mike." My father laces his fingers around his knee. "I agreed to this arrangement of yours because I wanted you to have a chance to find yourself while giving your sister time to settle into the role she'd chosen. Instead, just the opposite has happened. She's become a perpetual wreck and you seem more checked out than ever."

"Of course I've checked out. What d'you expect? She wanted to run the company and you just couldn't say no to her. You never could. So I made a different life for myself. Now that makes me the bad guy in all of this?"

"You're not the bad guy. But the company is going to need a full-time chief of operations."

"Yeah, she told me that." I uncross my legs. "Threatened to make a big deal about it over the holiday, too. That's why I didn't show up."

"Really?" He sounds unconvinced.

"I agreed not to fight her for control of the company." I meet his eyes without flinching. "I never agreed to give up my money. *That* was not the deal. And I will fight tooth and nail before she gets her way on that one."

"Damn it." Dad slaps the arm of the chair. "Why the hell can't the two of you work together?"

"Because she lacks vision." It's the truth. "Janet is a financial mastermind. She can tell to the penny if the money's going to work out on an opportunity better than anyone. She just can't see the opportunity until somebody puts it under her nose."

My father's face grimaces into a mask of defeat. He knows it's true. Better than anyone.

"So if I agreed to let you become CEO, would you come back tomorrow, full-time?"

"You'd never go through with it. Besides, Janet wouldn't let that happen without a fight. And I just don't want to fight with her, Dad."

"Mike, your sister is unhappy."

"And you think tossing her off the CEO track and installing me instead will put her in a happy place?" I shake my head in bewilderment. "Things are tense enough around here. There would never any peace if that happened."

"Think about it." Dad persists after a long pause. "In the meantime, keep your corporate salary. We'll work something else out."

"Thanks, Dad." I stand. "This means a lot to me."

"It should." He gives me a quick, fatherly hug. "Staying for lunch?"

"Can't. I need to get back." I scan his desk. "I'm sure you've got a lot to do, too."

As I reach for the door, he calls out to me. His words stop me cold.

"I know you didn't go to Mexico alone."

My hand stills on the door. "You have someone checking up on me?" It wouldn't be the first time.

"Not at all." He stands, turning to face me. "You didn't answer your cell, so I called the resort. When I asked to speak with you, they were politely informative."

"Okay. I wasn't alone." I rest my hands on my hips. "So what?"

"Is this someone I should know about?"

"I'll get back to you on that."

He stares at my stoic face for a few moments. "You do that."

"Goodbye, Dad."

"Bye, son."

There's something odd about his voice. It makes me pause for a second. Just one. Then I open the door and leave the room.

ZOE

"HELLO." I KNOCK ON THE FAMILIAR HOTEL DOOR OF ST. Rafe's. "Mike? It's Zoe."

It's been a few weeks since we returned from our vacation, and other than a few how's-it-going texts between us, Mike and I haven't seen each other. I'd started to worry that my request to slow down was being interpreted as girl code for leave me alone. Phone in hand, I'd started to call him when he beat me to it.

On Tuesday, he asked me to meet him at St. Rafe's on Saturday.

When the deadbolt clicks, I smooth my new red dress from Mexico.

"Hey." Mike leans against the doorjamb and eyes me up and down. "You look good."

"So do you." It's the truth. He's wearing linen pants and a light blue shirt. His button-down collar is damp from the wet hair on his neck and open in the front, revealing his perfect six-pack abs and sculpted chest.

"Come in." He opens the door wide and I scoot in under his arm.

The room has a sterile familiarity that makes me shiver. As I approach the small seating area by the window, Mike's luggage occupies one of the chairs. The high-end suitcase and laptop bag are a sharp contrast to the beat-up looking gym bag on the floor. I give a short laugh before taking the seat next to them.

"What?" Mike asks, walking up behind me.

"Why did you want to meet here?"

"Because we both like it here." He shrugs and sits on the corner of the bed near his shoes. "And it's neither here nor there. We can... do what we want, say what we want, without worrying about anyone or anything else. At least for a few hours at a time."

"Do you have your own place?" I ask.

"Yes. But in the interest of taking things slow, we can wait on that one. And since we can't go to your house and have any real privacy, this is a great middle ground. For now."

As I watch him slide on a pair of rugged looking closed-toe sandals, I think about what he's said and what I want to do next.

"Are you ready?" He looks up when he's done.

"Not yet," I decide.

"Yeah?" he gives me a wolfish smile.

I shake my head gently before reaching into the large, oversized purse I brought with me. It contains a change of clothes, some toiletries, and *this*.

"Before we go, I—I wanted to give you something," I tell him.

He looks surprised as I get up from the chair, walk over to the bed and present a brick-red leather box with a white bow. I stand in front of him, hold the box out nervously and smile.

"Um, there's no way I could ever pay for Mexico. And I know you know that. Still, though…" Damn, this probably isn't making much sense. "I wanted to give you something in return." My hand shakes and the bow dangles in front of him. "To say thank you. To say, I'm glad we went."

Mike's eyes are round with surprise as looks up at me and then back at the tiny box.

"Take it. Please," I tell him after a moment of awkward silence.

His fingers brush mine as he removes the box from my outstretched palm. A moment later he slips the white ribbon off and snaps it open. I watch as his thumb glides along the edge of the solid chrome watchcase. He pulls the watch from the box, studies the band and then turns it over.

"Where did you get this?" His voice sounds strange.

"A… vintage resale shop." I flush with embarrassment. Mike's not a secondhand store kind of guy, but I wanted to get him something special. And true to form, this special store delivered.

"Do you know what this is?"

"It's a Cuervo Sobrinos Habana watch. It's from the forties. You need to wind it manually, though." I point out the screw on the side of the face. "You always wear really nice watches, so I thought you might like this one, even if it is a little old-fashioned."

Mike cradles the watch in his lap, while one hand covers his mouth as he stares at it. The vibe in here is suddenly weird. He doesn't seem happy, sad…or anything. After a long silence, he looks up at me.

"This is really nice. Thank you, Zoe." His voice is stilted and a bit stoic, but his face tells another story.

"Oh, my god. Are you going to cry?" I kneel down to look at his face when he turns away.

"Of course not." A single tear wells in his bright blue eye.

"What's wrong?"

He lets me wipe a solitary tear from his thick dark brown eyelashes with the pad of my thumb.

"What's happening?" I'm stunned. Of all the reactions I'd expected, this was not on the short-list. "Mike?"

"I never get gifts, Zoe." He sounds distant.

"Ever? Come on. That doesn't make any sense."

"But it's true. Once people know my…situation, they assume I don't need anything, or if I do, I'll just buy it myself." He shrugs and picks up the box. "This is beautiful. I collect these, you know."

"I didn't know." I stroke his cheek, soothing it and checking for more tears. Relief shoots through me when there are none. "I just thought you'd like it."

"That's what makes it special. That and the fact that I know this was a lot for you, both in terms of time and expense." He plants a sweet kiss on my forehead. "It's nice that you went to the trouble."

"I wanted to do it, so it wasn't any trouble. And why would I give you something you wouldn't want or like? That makes no sense."

"It does in my world. People give me things all the time, but it's stuff they want me to have." Mike unclasps the metallic TAG Hauer he's wearing and slips his new watch out of the box.

"How does that work?" I ask, watching him weave the old-fashioned leather band into the buckle.

"They want me to wear something to a high profile venue, so they give it to me. They want me to drive a car so others in my circle ask me about it. I get to try out a lot of high-end autos on weekends, did you know that? Or my personal favorite—they need investor financing for this next big thing." Mike turns his wrist over and smiles at the watch. "Shit that has nothing to do with me."

Wow. My family, in contrast, doesn't have a lot, but we do try to make special occasions special. This is the first time I've felt sorry for someone for having more than we do.

I lace my fingers through his and turn his hand over to look at the watch. A good choice, I decide. "It looks good, Mike."

"So do you." Mike pulls me up between his knees and kisses me.

This is far from our first kiss, but it's definitely one-of-a-kind. It's a strange mix of urgency and tenderness, passion and restraint, familiar and new at the same time. It all comes complete with that ever-present chemistry neither of us ever got good at pretending didn't exist.

"Zo-Zo," he rasps the newly minted nickname in my ear. "You look so beautiful right now, with that hot red dress and your hair all blown out."

"Tha-ank you," I murmur between kisses.

"But as pretty as you are, I don't want to take you out." His hand slides down my waist and rests on my hip. "I want to peel this dress off, crawl into bed with you, and have a night we'll both remember for a long, long time."

I pull my face away, then slide my hands under his shirt along the smooth skin of his well-developed chest.

"You're killing me."

I watch his throat work hard as he swallows. I press a kiss to the base of his throat. I stand and smooth the shirt off his shoulders and down his arms. Mike rises, lifting me up with him. His mouth finds the curve of my shoulder and kisses a trail up to my neck. He maneuvers behind me, his lips never leaving me while he unzips he back of my dress.

My clothes land in a crumpled heap on the floor. Mike carries me to the bedside and drops me on the firm mattress. His gaze skates over my body, taking in the strapless bra and matching thong.

"Mike..."

"We don't need to say anything, Zo-Zo. Unless you want to stop."

I shake my head.

He removes his crisp, ironed shirt and tosses it onto the chair. His eyes stare into mine, unwavering, and once again, I'm overcome with the feeling that something's changed. When we've been together before, he projected an air of eager, amused confidence.

Now he stands in front of me with a feral, impatient look on his face. It evokes an excited hunger in me.

I kneel on the mattress at the side of the bed, kissing the center of his chest while running my hands up and down his torso. The hurried unbuckling of his belt and the rushed, shrill sound of his zipper follow before he steps out of his pants, then peels off his underwear as his sandals hit the floor in successive clops.

He climbs up on the bed and we're so close to the headboard there's no place for me to go except against the wall.

"Stay like this," he insists, turning me to face the wall with his hand planted firmly on my hip.

I look over my shoulder and watch as he reaches for his wallet on the bedside table. A rushed, rapid ripping of a foil condom wrapper fills the air as Mike puts the corner in his mouth and pulls, then drops the opened pack onto the pillow next to my bent knee.

"Zo-Zo." He caresses my breast with one hand while he pulls the strap of my thong to one side with the fingers of his other. Before when we were together, the tenderness of his kisses ebbed and flowed until our desires synced. Now his pace is urgent, rushed, demanding.

Mike moves his fingers along the back of my thong, fondling the folds leading to my intimate core. He quickly finds the most sensitive, aroused places, then shows me no mercy as he strokes and explores until my hips push back along his fingers.

"Good." He sounds pleased. "Just like that."

Mike's hand leaves my breasts and reaches for the foil pack on the bed. He braces his erection against my hip and rolls the condom down his bulging shaft with one hand while his other strokes me with fierce urgency.

"Ah-h." I react as his fingers work their skilled magic inside me.

"Now, Zo-Zo." With a hand on each of my hips, Mike pulls me back from the wall, impaling me with a single fluid motion. His grip on my hips is solid as he adds momentum to my own thrusts. His strokes become powerful and unrelenting, a tacit reminder of his physical strength.

"Come for me," Mike pleads. "Soon. Please."

This part is easy. My heart races, my blood pressure spikes, and my breathing becomes a series of broken pants. And all at once, I shatter inside.

As my pulsing folds push against him, Mike's thrusts become faster, more insistent. The sensation of him inside me changes subtly, and seconds later he follows me down this familiar path.

But this time, something's different.

Mike's forehead collapses near my shoulder blades. As his orgasm ebbs, he makes a guttural sound that's so low it's almost a growl. He's never made that sound before. A strange mix of satisfaction, relief, and peace. Both primal and flattering, I don't think I've ever heard anything quite like it.

"Mine. All mine." His big powerful body curls around me and he kisses my shoulder as we fall together into a state of semi-conscious bliss.

MIKE

"GODDAMN IT, WHAT THE HELL WAS THAT?" RODGERS rants from ringside.

I suppress the urge to smile and trash-talk the Madman as my left hook catches his chin. Usalv looks stunned, but I can't tell if it's the force of the blow or the fact that it connected.

Damn, I'm on fire. And it's all because of Zoe.

We had an incredible weekend together. Spent the night at St. Rafe's, with breakfast at the terrace restaurant. Then we drove along the shore of Lake Michigan heading north. Stopped for a late lunch-early dinner at some marina along the way before heading back to the city. I don't know what the hell we talked about, but we never stopped. When we had checked the time, neither of us could believe how late it was. I dropped her off around nine-thirty Sunday night.

The thing about Zoe is she jumps into life. Whether she's working, or making love, or going to bat for people she cares about, the woman is all-in and out loud about it. I want to be like that, live like that, feel like that. And I want her around to show me how.

Yes! My round kick strikes the muscular portion of Madman's thigh. Goddamn, I'm *good*.

"Fuck." Madman grunts.

"Okay, okay guys." Rodgers huffs. "Let's wrap it up. We all know what we need to know today."

We relax our stances, and I look over at Usalv. As much fun as this was, he's not in top form today.

"Hey, Madman." I clap him on the shoulder.

"Mike." He's bent at the waist, trying to catch his breath.

I hesitate for a minute. "You good?"

His laugh is flat. "I've been better."

"Damn." I rest my hands on my waist. "I was hoping it was all me."

"A lot of it was. You definitely brought your A-game today."

He's always been a good guy, even when things aren't going his way.

"How's Louise?" I realize too late that it was the wrong question to ask.

Madman stands straight up and stares me down. "I'm not trying to piss you off, Mike. But we're really good. I didn't steal her from you. She was never yours."

Damn. Strange as it sounds, I'd forgotten about my mad crush on Louise. It seems so long ago now. The fact is, after meeting Zoe at Paul's party, I haven't thought about Louise at all.

"I know." I sound honest and calm. "And I'm sorry. For real." My gloved hand extends a vertical fist.

"Thanks," he replies, jabbing his fist into mine.

"Usalv?" Rodgers bellows from his perch by the ring. "Come on over."

"Fuck. Here it comes," he tells me. "I better go."

"Sure. See you, Madman."

"Yeah." He shoots me a confused look. "Take it easy, Mike."

I lean through the ropes of the ring, and Rodgers gives me a curt nod of approval. I'm trying to savor the moment when Doug catches up with me as I walk toward the locker room.

"Great job today, Mike." He claps me on the back.

"Thanks." I shrug. "To be fair, the Madman isn't at his best right now."

"Maybe you aren't either." Doug slows to a stop outside the corridor.

"What?" I stop next to him.

"Have you thought about switching weight classes like I've told you?"

"Not really. I'm six-foot-two, and I go at about two-twenty-five."

"Yeah, but what's your body fat percentage? You look somewhere between eight and twelve percent."

"Probably. It's an easy weight for me to maintain, and there's no real advantage to being lighter in this division. In fact, just the opposite is true."

"That's why I think it's time you took things to the next level," Doug insists. "If you're twelve percent at two-twenty-five, that's twenty-seven pounds. Half of that is about fourteen pounds. That puts you at two-eleven and six percent. Just six pounds away from light heavyweight."

"Yeah, and about four percent body fat."

"We both know plenty of guys that fight at four percent," Doug reminds me. "And you only need to be that weight for the official weigh-in."

"That's true." For the first time, I start to consider it.

"You're strong. You're fast. Faster than most heavy-weights. But you're not as big as the top guys. Hell, Madman's a beast. He probably fights at between six and eight percent, and he's still north of two-forty." Doug looks back at where Coach and Madman are talking. "Light heavyweight might be a better match for your skills."

It'll be a huge bitch, losing that much weight. Strict diets, more aerobic workouts. But for the first time in a long while, I don't feel stuck in neutral. I always felt bad about the family business. I started MMA training because I could see things weren't going to go my way with Dad and Janet. And the hell of it is, it's not like she's a bad choice to run the company.

After the Great Recession that no politician even acknowledges happened anymore, the property business was a fucking minefield. Janet, a newly minted MBA from a top school, had the knowledge without baggage to know which of our properties to hold or fold on. Everyone thinks she saved our asses. I can't blame them for feeling that way. After all, she learned the business sitting on the same knees I did, taking it all in from a young age.

We see the same things. We just don't see them the same way.

It's time for me to start taking the life I've chosen for myself seriously. No one else is going to unless I do it first.

"Let's give it a try, Doug. See where it takes us."

"Great. That's fucking great." Doug slaps my shoulder. "I can hook you up with a nutritionist. We can get started in the next day or so."

"Looking forward to it."

ZOE

"Zoe?" Chloe knocks on the bathroom door.

"Yeah?" I answer just before brushing my teeth.

"Can you take me to the doctor's? I was supposed to go the last week of June but I had to cancel."

A wave of cold heat sends shockwaves up my spine, causing the hairs on the back of my neck to stand straight up. My toothbrush drops into the sink as my hands fly to the medicine cabinet door and rip it open.

A single light purple box is wedged between the side of the cabinet and a bottle of Tylenol. I grasp the box and squeeze it open, then slap it against my hand until a foil-covered square slides onto my palm.

No. No, no, no, no. NO.

My palms are sweaty, and I feel faint as I sit down on the toilet. After several deep breaths, I gently plunge my fingers inside my intimate parts. Seconds later, I pull out my contraceptive ring. My *old* contraceptive ring.

"Zoe?" Chloe knocks again. "Is that okay? Can you take me?"

"Why didn't you go when you were supposed to?" My voice is a mixture of anger and panic.

"There was a last-minute schedule change at work, and I needed the extra hours. Then I was going to do it during the holiday week, but they were closed on the days you were gone, and I wanted you to take me."

"Is this for your contraceptive shot?" I ask, staring at the useless device in my hand.

"Yeah, but no worries. I'm still on the V-team and I'm not even messing around with anyone," she tells me from other side of the door. "Like you said. It's just a precaution."

"You need to keep those appointments, Chloe. Make sure you get those shots on time." I pull open the cabinet doors underneath the bathroom sink and start rummaging.

"Hey, are you okay in there?" she asks.

"Yeah. I'm fine." I pull out a pregnancy test from behind an old cleaning bucket. I shiver as all the things I've put into place as precautionary measures are dragged out into the light of day.

For *my* use.

I've always worried that Chloe or I would get pregnant too young, like our mom. My mother, to her credit, never objected to safe sex or delaying pregnancy. In high school, I was so driven and determined to do well I didn't even have a steady boyfriend. She'd tolerated having these precautions around because she knew we had no real need for them.

As I nurse, I've always had access to the latest knowledge and supplies, so she's let me advise Chloe on these things, too.

"Zoe, are you going to be in there a while?"

"Yes. I'm taking a shower." I tear the wrapper from the pregnancy test stick. "Make sure your appointment is on a day I don't work. Then text me the time, okay?"

"Thanks, Zoe."

It's the last thing she says before I turn on the shower and sit back down.

My contraceptive ring should've been changed the week after I returned from Mexico. Chloe's appointments help me remember. But she had canceled, then forgot, and I did, too. It simply stayed in. The problem is, the hormones run out, and without the hormones there's no birth control protection.

My temples throb as I put the pregnancy stick between my legs and pee. When I'm satisfied that the tip is good and soaked, I lay it over the edge of the bathroom counter. Then I step into the shower for possibly the last few minutes of life as I know it.

Under the rush of steamy water, I try to calm down and clear my head, two things at cross purposes right now. I pump a few shots of shower gel into my hands and rub it along the curves of my body, and my panicked brain starts to recall physical symptoms of pregnancy I've experienced but ignored.

The breast tenderness I'd chalked up to new lingerie purchased in Mexico. The extreme fatigue blamed on hectic shifts and the summer heat. The waves of morning nausea that mimicked a stomach bug. I caress the slight swelling above my pelvic triangle, which I'd blamed on rich foods indulged in on vacation.

Do I really need to count lines on a stick?

My body languishes in the shower until the hot water disappears. Then I languish more until it becomes unbearably frigid. After shutting off the water, I scrub my skin dry until it hurts with my faded blue towel before wrapping it around my tender breasts.

I take a deep breath, then step out of the shower.

The pregnancy stick hangs over the edge of the counter. Two lines are clearly visible in the plastic window, confirming what's obvious by now. I fling it violently into the trash, where it bounces off the plastic wastebasket with a vicious snap.

Then I open the door and hurry into my room to dress for work.

"Zoe?" Chloe's voice is strange as she knocks on my bedroom door. "Can I come in, please?"

"Sure." I'm lying on top of my comforter, wearing today's work scrubs. I stroke my stomach while staring at the ceiling.

She closes the door behind her with one hand while the other remains stuffed in the front pocket of her hoodie. She holds up something wrapped in Kleenex and her eyes meet mine with a terrified expression.

"What is it?" I shift onto my hip and watch her.

"Don't be mad." She approaches my bed and sits beside me. "But I found this in the trash when I emptied it." Chloe removes the toilet paper from around the pregnancy stick and tosses it onto my bed.

"Damn. My head wasn't straight when I tossed it in there. Sorry, Chloe."

"You don't need to be sorry." She pauses. "Is it Mike's?"

"Yeah. It's his."

"That's good." She blows out a breath. "Isn't it?"

"I'm not sure yet." My voice seethes with brutal honesty.

"Are you going to take the morning-after pill?" she asks.

"It's too late for that," I explain. "This happened in Mexico. I've been pregnant for over a month now."

"Oh." She hesitates again. "Does he know?"

"No."

"Are... you going to tell him?"

"Not yet."

"Why not?"

"Because this was a total birth control failure that was completely unplanned." I curl my arm around my stomach.

"Are you afraid he'll be mad?"

"There's always that possibility." I acknowledge. "But it's more because I don't know how *I* feel about this. And until I do, there's no room in my life for somebody else telling me how I should feel or what I should do."

"I won't say anything." Chloe lays her hand on top of mine, which still cradles my stomach. "But you can't hide it forever. And if you keep it, I think you'd be a great mom."

'Oh god, Chloe. I screwed up so bad." Tears well in my eyes as I start to sob.

"No, you didn't." She strokes my hair. "You graduated high school. You went to college. You have a job that pays good money. You take care of the house. You take of *me*." Her voice breaks, but she recovers quickly. "What happened between you and Mike... That's what's *supposed* to happen."

"Please be careful Chloe," I warn her irrationally. "Don't let this happen to you."

"You worry about *you*." Her voice becomes stern. "I am careful. But nobody's got the lockdown on how things turn out. Not even you, Big Sis."

I lie there wailing on my bed, trying to muffle my tears, while my younger sister strokes my hair.

"Settle down," she tells me after a few minutes. "This isn't good for either of you."

Then, without warning, she climbs into the bed and cradles me from behind, shushing me like a colicky baby.

"Thank you," I murmur.

"You're welcome."

MIKE

"She looks good, Macy." We enter the hospital elevator on the seventh floor. "They're taking good care of her. But you already know that."

"It's true," she replies. "But it's hard to see her like that. She's such a strong person."

I rub Macy's upper back and squeeze her shoulder. "She'll get through this."

Macy nods and wipes a tear from her eye. "She will. Thanks for being here, Mike."

"I'm here for both of you."

Louise, Macy's best friend and former roommate, was hurt in a street attack, and she's been in the hospital for over a week. It's a well-known fact that I had a big thing for Louise until she moved in with Usalv. He's a good friend, so I was pissed at both of them over it. But looking back on the way things turned out, I'm glad it happened.

If Usalv hadn't beaten the shit out of me, I wouldn't have met Zoe.

When Macy had told me she was visiting Louise on her breaks, it made sense for me to ask if I could come along. We've all known each other for a long time, and I wanted to be supportive without making things awkward for anyone.

"It's nice that you came to see her today," Macy tells me. "Staying in a hospital can be a real downer, especially if you're here a while."

"She'll be home soon." My response is distracted as my thoughts turn to Zoe. Is she working today?

"Mike." Macy holds my arm as the elevator doors open onto the first floor. "Are you okay?"

"Yeah. I'm good." I pull away to step outside the elevator.

"I was a little worried when Louise told me about the fight you got into with Usalv," she follows me out.

"I know they're together now, Macy. And I'm okay with that." The elevator shuts and I look around the hallway. We're alone for the moment but that won't last. "I squared things with Usalv, and we've both moved on. Do me a favor? Talk to Louise and let her know everything's fine."

"I can do that. Sure." Macy starts to say something else, but both of us feel more than see someone moving quickly toward us.

Macy turns and watches as a thirty-five-is looking woman wearing maroon scrubs and a short white lab coat approaches us. The frames of her eyeglasses coordinate perfectly with the maroon scrubs, and her long corn-row braids are pulled away from her face in a large ponytail.

"Who's that?" I ask.

"Hell on wheels," Macy answers. "My boss."

"Macy," the woman's voice is elevated. "I know your friend is sick. And I'm sorry about that, really, but you need to get back to work."

"Sorry, Renece," Macy tells her when she stops in front of us. "Zoe is supposed to be covering for me. Isn't she there?"

Renece rolls her eyes, lifting her brows above the frames of her glasses. "Zoe's in the bathroom, throwing up like a frat house plebe after a rush party."

"Oh, my god. Is she sick?" Macy asks.

Renece checks out the hallway and waits for a few people to pass. "I think she's pregnant."

"What?" Macy and I say at the same time.

Renece and Macy both shoot me an odd, puzzled look.

"Wow, how can you just know like that? Maybe she's got a stomach bug," I stammer in an awkward voice.

"How do I know?" Renece puts one hand on her waist and gives me an assessing look. "I've got three kids. Two of them came after I became a nurse. And I've treated a lot of pregnancies in my day. How do I know a pregnant woman when I see one? Wait for it... I've got to count out how many ways."

I feel the urge to say something when Macy reaches out and grabs my forearm. "I should go, Mike. Can we talk later?"

Her intervention snaps me out of it. "Of course." I manage a mechanically normal nod. "I'll leave you to it." I look over at Renece, give her a goodbye smile, then step toward the elevator and push the button.

Over my shoulder I watch as they hurry down the corridor, speaking in muffled whispers. When the elevator door opens, it's empty. It's not obvious what a relief it is until I lean against the wall and try to catch my breath.

Zoe can NOT be pregnant.

We might be spontaneous and impulsive, but we've been pretty careful, all things said and done.

Besides, she would tell me. Right?

I push myself off the elevator wall, stand straight up, and take out my cellphone. I'm running late this morning and need to invite Zoe to St. Rafe's for the weekend. It's become a great treat for us. When the elevator doors open, I send her a text.

Meet me at St. Rafe's? Sat. night, usual time.

There's no answer as I enter the lower level into the hospital parking lot. My Range Rover idles for a few minutes while I await a response.

Nothing. Maybe being underground is interfering with the cell phone signal?

I snap my cellphone into its dashboard holder before pulling out. My motions are mechanical as I drive to the parking lot exit and insert my ticket and pay. During every pause of those monotonous steps, I constantly check my cell phone for new text messages.

Nothing.

Damn it. My game plan for today was scheduled site

visits, which entitled me to use of one of the company drivers. But if my day ended at Zoe's house, her address on a paper trail wasn't a good idea, especially with Janet watching me like a hawk.

Gold coast traffic is a bitch at this time of day, so going home is less than ideal at the moment. And as for site visits, those can wait for another time. Without thinking too much about it, I merge onto the expressway heading north out of the city. After setting the cruise control, I scan the phone propped up on the dash for texts.

Still nothing.

Maybe this is all one big fucking false alarm. Maybe Zoe's just sick. Maybe Renece doesn't know what the hell she's talking about. After all, suppose it was true. How, when, could it have happened?

The waterfall.

My memories take me there in an instant. Neither one of us had brought any condoms. At that point, I was pretty sure she'd cut me off. But then we just couldn't help ourselves. She'd told me before that she used hormonal birth control, so I hadn't worried about it. Other than that time, we've been extremely diligent.

As I merge into the far left lane, my thoughts cloud with doubt. Why wouldn't she tell me? Fuck. If I'm fair, there's a million reasons. Maybe she's afraid I'll tell her to get rid of it. Or insist that she keep it. Maybe she's worried that I'll want to break up with her. Or stay with her just for the kid's sake. She does have a lot of baggage in that department.

My eyes dart to my phone again. Nothing.

Well, assuming she knows, and she must know…
One, because she's a nurse. Two, because, well… Zoe
knows better than anyone how she's been spending her
off-hours… Maybe she just needs some time to process
and sort her own feelings out about it.

Speaking of which, how do I feel about
being…a dad?

I grip the steering wheel tight as my brain toys with
the possibility, waiting to be overwhelmed by a rush of
heated panic. But it never comes.

I've always pictured myself being a dad one day.
Never doubted it, in fact. Although I've never been clear
on the particulars, like my age at the time, or gender
preference, let alone anything about their mother, I've
always known it would happen.

Maybe this is the way things are supposed to work
out for me?

I break out into a smile. Driving along in a calm state
of acceptance, I check the exit number and realize I've
overshot my parents' place by a good ten minutes. It
makes me laugh.

The phone buzzes at an incoming text message. The
car's Bluetooth system roars to life, displaying Zoe's
message on the console.

Sorry, not this weekend.

Damn it. "Siri?" I speak out loud to my iPhone.

"I'm here," the phone responds.

"Text," I order it.

"To whom should I send your message?"

"Zoe."

"Why not?" I say out loud.

"Do you want me to send it?" Siri asks.

"Send."

Not feeling well. Zoe responds.

Something about her answer doesn't sit well with me. It's only Tuesday. How can she possibly know how she's going to feel on Friday? Unless of course, she knows what's wrong.

Gee, wonder would it could be?

And just like that, I *know* two things. One that's she pregnant and two, that she's avoiding me. I look out the rearview window and jerk my car over onto the shoulder of the highway.

Everything okay? I text furiously after ripping my phone out of its holder.

No answer.

Zoe? I ask after a few minutes of non-communication.

Talk.

To.

Me. I send three separate texts.

Sorry. Just need some time… To rest, I think.

Is there anything I can do? I punch out the words.

Not right now… see you, okay? I'm at work.

Sure. Talk later.

Okay…

My temples throb as cars whiz passed me on the highway. She needs to tell me, the sooner the better. But I can't confront her, either. The way I found out is totally fucked up, and I could get the people she works with in real trouble, especially Macy.

But it is not acceptable that she doesn't tell me, and

for me to forget I knew. It's my baby too, and I can't pretend it doesn't exist. No. Zoe's got to tell me, and I've got to persuade her.

In fact, I've got to make it very difficult for her *not* to tell me.

ZOE

"MIKE?" I CAN'T HIDE MY SURPRISE. "WHAT ARE YOU doing here?"

"Checking up on you," he answers with a half-joking, half-serious expression.

As he leans against the front jamb, I bristle in confusion and agitation, suddenly grateful for my baggy sweatshirt and pants. My swelling abdomen underneath is hardly visible, but with all the time we've spent naked together, he's the person most likely to detect any change.

"You don't need to do that," I tell him.

"Of course not. But I was worried. After all, you've been sick for a whole week. How are you feeling?"

How do I feel? That's a good question.

Dazed. Ambivalent. Guilty.

Dazed because I'm still processing the new reality of impending motherhood. Ambivalent because I don't know what to do next. Guilty because I want to feel happy, to enjoy this baby. But being pregnant changes things a lot. And not just for me.

Chloe. Mom. Mike.

"I'm a little worn down," I answer.

"Typical nurse," he chides.

"What's that supposed to mean?" *Who do I behave like?*

"Nurses don't take good care of themselves when they're sick. For some reason, basic medical wisdom doesn't apply to them."

This conversation upsets me. There's too much truth and too many underlying questions that come to mind. I want to tell him that I'm going to bed, but the smell of hot chicken broth gets my attention.

"What's that?" I nod toward two large brown paper sacks that Mike holds by their corded handles.

"Didn't you get my text?" He sounds disappointed.

"Must have nodded off. Sorry."

"Sweet potato ravioli with sage and brown butter. Sautéed endive. Italian wedding soup. Tiramisu." He raises the bags up, causing their delicious smells to mingle in the late evening air. "There's even enough to share with your mom and sister."

"Mom's working. Chloe's out, doing whatever teenagers do in the summer right before senior year starts."

"More for us then." Mike shrugs. "Can I come in?"

I should say no, make some excuse and ask him to leave. It doesn't feel right to tell him about the baby now, but at the same time, it feels wrong to keep it a secret.

"You might get sick," I offer lamely.

"Zoe, I'm not going to get what you have. Trust me."

My face flushes. Is it shock? Embarrassment? Both? I turn away from him, toward the inside of the house and somehow manage to lose my balance. Mike drops the bags and grabs my arm to steady me.

"Hey, you okay, Zo-Zo?" His other arm reaches around my waist.

"Fine." His arm feels good around me. "Just a little clumsy."

"Have you eaten anything? I know your sister tries, but she's a rotten cook."

"That's not very nice."

"Answer my question."

"No, I haven't eaten."

"Clumsy my ass." Without any warning, Mike scoops me up in his arms. With his strong hand around my back and the other under my bent knees, he sidesteps the takeout bags and kicks the front door shut behind us. "It's all settled."

"What is?" I gasp as he carries me into the living room.

"I'm taking care of you tonight." His voice is an impatient bark. He looks around our small entryway then heads to the couch. "Starting with feeding you dinner."

"You don't have to do that," I complain. "I can take care of myself."

"Of course you can." Mike takes a deep breath then places me gently on the couch. "But maybe I want to. Is that okay?"

The quiet intensity of gaze and words make me

wonder if he's talking about something else. But it's probably just my imagination running away with me and all my problems. After all, what else could it be?

"That's fine." My voice is hoarse. "Thank you."

"You're welcome." He covers my legs with the old blanket lying next to me, then drops a gentle kiss on my forehead. "Rest while I fix you a plate. Is there anything that you don't want to eat?"

"No. It all sounded great."

"Good." He stands up and looks at our tiny television. "Oh, by the way, I brought my iPad with me. There's a movie downloaded on it that we can watch."

"That's nice. We don't have cable or Wi-Fi. We just use our cell phones or the antenna."

"We don't even need that. It's loaded onto the device. Just press play," he tells me before leaving the room. A few minutes later, he returns with an iPad that looks as big as our TV. He places it on the coffee table and opens the app up for me.

"That was very thoughtful." I start to relax and allow myself to enjoy the evening. The truth is, spending time with Mike always feels good and I don't want to be alone. It's so easy to let him take over and right now that's more than okay. "What's it called?"

"The Back-up Plan."

MIKE

"WHAT'S THAT?" ZOE ASKS.

"It's a chick flick, isn't it?" My response is deliberately slow as I fumble through the takeout bags. "It's got J. Lo in it, and the main character's name is Zoe, too. Something for both of us."

"I take it you're a J. Lo fan?" she asks from the couch in an amused tone.

"I'm a Zoe fan. J. Lo.'s easy on the eyes, but I wouldn't say she's turned me into a chick flick junkie. You should take advantage of the fact you're not feeling well and I'm trying hard to make you comfortable."

"Thanks." Zoe gives a laughing huff.

Does she know I heard her?

I bring the plates out to her. When Zoe sees me, she moves her feet off the couch onto the coffee table. I settle next to her, and the sides of our legs touch each other.

"I'm not *that* hungry Mike." She stares at the plate I hand her.

"Sure you are. Every time I'm with you, you eat like it's been a week since you've had a meal."

"That's not very nice." She sounds offended.

"Maybe not, but it's true. Your mom tends bar?" I ask.

"What does that have to do with anything?"

"She gets to eat at work, doesn't she?"

"Yes."

"And I know your sister tries, but she's a lousy cook."

She's about to protest, but I give her my best disarming smile. "Just relax and watch the movie."

I fidget with my tablet until she takes a few bites. When she looks comfortable, I press play and place the iPad on the coffee table between us.

The opening scene features movie-Zoe chatting in neurotic fashion to her doctor while she undergoes a gynecological exam.

"I'll elevate your legs for ten minutes and then you're good to go," the movie-doctor says.

"Christ. Spare me that." I tell her.

"What? The stirrups? I think you're safe, Mike."

"Not that." A freaky image flashes through my mind. "I mean having to do so much just to have a child. I hope it's not that hard for me—"

Beside me, Zoe chokes on her food. As in damn, do I need to do the Heimlich maneuver? I never intended to make her suffer, only to compel her to confide in me.

"Oh, my god. Are you okay?" I ask, after an eternal minute of hacking.

"Fine," she croaks. "Wa, water—"

I reach over her and grab a glass from the side table. She takes a few desperate greedy gulps and tries to collect herself.

"Better?"

She seems to settle. "How embarrassing," she replies. "I'm fine. Let's eat dinner and watch."

"Okay." I settle back into my seat on the couch, hyper-aware of Zoe next to me.

As the movie continues, Zoe displays a wide range of emotions. She goes from picking at her food to giving up entirely. She smiles when the couple meets, laughs at some of the more ridiculous women in the single mommy club. But as the relationship between movie-Zoe and her true love blossoms, my Zo-Zo stiffens against me.

"Everything okay?" I ask.

"Sure. It's only a movie, right?" Zoe leans forward and plops the half-eaten dinner on the coffee table, then folds her arms and sinks back into the overstuffed couch.

"Yeah. Right," I answer. My arm slips around her shoulders and I draw her close to me. She hesitates a moment but doesn't resist.

As things move along, I worry that maybe this wasn't such a good idea. Sure, I'd watched the movie before bringing it here tonight. But now, sitting beside Zoe, feeling her emotional tension erupt like a silent volcano, her stressed-out state affects me.

When we get to the live birth scene in the apartment, I lose it, too.

"Oh god," I groan, as movie-Zoe faints into the bodily fluid-laden baby pool. "Please tell me you're not into this at home, do-it-yourself childbirth stuff."

"Hell, no," she insists. "I'm having mine at a major medical facility with real doctors and real drugs."

"Thank god we agree on that," I speak the words before I can check myself.

"What? Why is that good?" she asks in a panicked voice.

Oh shit.

"Well…you know."

"No, I don't."

"If things go well…it helps to know we share certain points of view."

"Do you want children?" She sounds surprised.

"Sure. I mean, I've never been the type of guy who's been on the fence about it. Should I or shouldn't I? That's not me. It's the details that have always left me hanging."

"The details?"

"Who, what, when… You know, the details."

Zoe gives me a silent nod before drawing her knees into her chest. Her look of distress makes me feel like shit. I can't help myself. I put my arm around her and hold her close. "It's okay, Zo-Zo. Just watch the movie."

She relaxes, and so do I. It's possible my feelings about having children gave her some relief. But then the scene comes where movie-Zoe and her true love discover they're having twins. Zoe holds steady through that scene until...

"Are you sure you want to do this?" Movie-Zoe asks.

"I'm really sure," Mr. Perfect answers.

Beside me, Zoe leaps off the couch and bursts into tears.

"What is it, Zoe?" My voice is calm.

"Nothing, it's... nothing. It's so sad, though," Zoe replies through a waterfall of tears as she paces around the other side of the coffee table.

"What is? Why are you crying?"

"To be forced to choose between keeping your baby, and, and—"

"Yes?" I prompt.

Zoe swallows hard. "Someone you care about. A lot."

I look down at the iPad and then back at her. "But no one's making anyone choose. Besides, it's only a movie."

Zoe clutches her stomach and shakes her head. "No, it isn't, Mike."

ZOE

"WHAT DO YOU MEAN?" MIKE ASKS WITH A CALM, expectant expression.

As I watch Mike through a haze of tears, Chloe's warning comes back to haunt me. *You can't keep this a secret forever.* She was right. I knew it even then. But I didn't how, when, or where I would tell Mike about it.

Now it's clear.

What's frightened me all along is that I *really* like him. Mike's got his rough edges, just like the rest of us, but he's one of the kindest, most thoughtful people I've ever met. That doesn't even include all the amazing physical stuff. Since learning I was pregnant, my biggest fear has been that what had happened to my mother would happen to me.

That Mike would leave me because of our baby.

My father had left my mom when she became pregnant with me. While my childhood sucked in many ways, she'd never blamed me for my father's absence. It never occurred to me until this moment how brave she was, or what she'd given up to keep me.

I refuse to be less brave. Now or ever.

"Do you remember our trip to Mexico?" I ask, clearing my throat and wiping my tears to see him better.

"I'll never forget it," he replies, the joy in his tone undeniable.

"How about the day we hiked to the waterfall?"

"That was the highlight of my trip." Mike gives me a wolfish smile, but his eyes stay soft and focused.

"Well, you might not feel that way after I tell you what happened." Though my tone is somber, I can't quite keep the anxiety from my words.

"What happened?"

Damn, he's calm. I brace myself for a possible explosion.

"Neither one of us had condoms with us, so we relied on my hormonal birth control."

"I remember."

"Well," I swallow hard. "It didn't work."

His clear eyes study my teary ones. A look of comprehension flashes across his face and he breaks eye contact. He sits down on the couch with an inscrutable expression.

"I should've changed my contraceptive ring the week after we returned," I stammer. "Because of the holiday, and the vacation, other things, I... got confused and didn't." I take a deep breath. "I'm pregnant, Mike."

"I assume you're telling me this for a reason?" His voice is gentle. "Do you intend to keep the baby?"

"Yes. Despite my chaotic childhood, or maybe even

because of it, I've always wanted my own children." I sigh. "And while the timing is far from ideal, I have a good job, health insurance, and a place to live. In my world that's as good as it gets."

He studies me with a pensive look. "In my world, things are a little better than that."

"I'm not so sure. It's your baby, too. But I think it's best you decide if you want to be involved or not. You have time to think about it."

"What does that mean?" he asks.

"My point of view on this is unique." I take a deep breath as old wounds reopen. "My dad was not in the picture growing up. At all. From day one that's how it was. He was never interested in being a dad, and there's been next to no contact."

"Oh."

"The last time I saw my father was in my mid-teens. A mutual friend of my parents died and my mom and I went to the funeral together. He didn't even recognize me. When he asked who I was, Mom replied, *this is my Zoe.* He left quickly, wearing a look of disbelief. When I asked Mom who he was, she told me."

Mike remains silent for a moment. "I guess this is one of those things you warned me I'd find shocking about you."

"Maybe. My point is, not having a father sucked sometimes, sure. But I never carried the burden of false hope. Chloe's childhood has been completely different. Her dad is unstable and inconsistent. He's in and out of her life, and it's made Chloe an insecure wreck. She always wonders when and if he'll return, worried that somehow she drove him away."

"I'm so sorry for both of you."

"I'm not asking for pity, Mike. But for the baby's sake, either make a commitment to be in the picture or stay away. Don't pop in and out. It will make things hard. And life will be hard enough." I feel tears well in my eyes.

"Not for my child."

"What?"

He gets up from the couch and stands in front me, his hands on my shoulders. "Look at me."

I look up, fold my arms in front of me and stare into his eyes.

"I'm not some stupid, clueless teenager either." He pushes my chin up with a gentle brush of his fingers. "I know how babies get made and what happened in Mexico. I intend to be a father to my child."

My face breaks into a grateful smile and I collapse against his chest. Tears flow down my cheeks, soaking the front of his shirt. "Whatever happens between us, please don't desert our baby."

A strange sound rattles through his chest. "I don't think I could do that to either one of you. I like you a lot, Zoe. The baby doesn't change that."

Relief mixed with joy flood through me and my sobs come in irregular bursts as I circle my arms around his muscular torso. Mike kisses the top of my head, then slides his hands down to the crease where my thigh and backside meet. He squeezes me with a firm grip, lifting up and pulling me into his warm, rigid pelvis.

My hands slide up his arms until my fingers find the back of his neck and I pull his face down to mine. When our lips collide, we assail each other with pent up passion. Before tonight, I hadn't spoken with Mike in over a week, and it's been even longer since we've been together, at St. Rafe's or anywhere else.

Being away from him has been torture. I can always count on Mike to make me feel better, more optimistic, regardless of what's going on in my real life.

Oh, how I've missed that. How I've needed that.

"Um...Zoe?" he asks, gripping my hips as they thrust against him.

"Mmm?" I groan while continuing to kiss him.

"What are the...rules, now that you're pregnant?" Mike pulls me close to him, stilling my movements while he waits for my answer.

"The rules are that since the morning sickness ebbed, I'm more sexually amped up at the strangest times and most inconvenient places." My hips push against his hands, eager to resume their gyrations.

"Is that normal?" His tone brims with urgent curiosity.

"Yes. A fast-growing baby means a lot of physiolog-ical stuff is happening. Hormones, increased blood flow...all hypersensitize the already sensitive parts of the pelvic area."

"That's a good thing?"

"It is if you've got a way to deal with it." I'm growing impatient with this conversation, and grip his firm, muscular butt, pulling him into me.

Mike gives me a familiar, wolfish smile. "Maybe I can help you with that."

"You think?" I attempt to sound doubtful.

He takes a quick look around the house. "Where's your mom?"

"Working."

"Your sister?"

"Out."

"She coming back?"

"Curfew's eleven-thirty."

Mike glances down at his vintage watch and my breath hitches when I recognize it as my gift to him.

"I can definitely work with that."

I erupt into giggles. I clap him on his upper arm, which makes my palm sting.

"Ow," I whine and we both burst into laughter.

Mike takes my hand and soothes the soreness with a kiss. Then his tone becomes quiet and serious. "Where's your room, Zoe?"

"This way."

By the time we reach the bedroom, I've wrapped my legs around Mike's muscular waist. He carries me as he walks, kissing my neck and throat. As we cross the threshold of my door, he sets me down and kicks it shut.

He removes my long sweatshirt, pulling it above my head, revealing my topless chest beneath it. While his impatient fingers fumble with his shirt buttons, Mike backs me up against the bed. I scramble onto the mattress and up toward the headboard, leaving him plenty of room to join me.

I watch as Mike sheds the last of his clothes in a

heated rush before crawling slowly up the mattress like an eager predator that's cornered its prey.

He removes my lace-waist panties and parts my bent knees, then sits back and studies me while his gentle fingers brush the small swell of my lower abdomen. He cups the protruding baby bump in his gentle hands, testing it, squeezing the edges around my stomach before rubbing it with smooth, soothing swirls.

"Are you sure it's okay?" he asks.

"Don't worry." I give him a reassuring smile. "Well-endowed as you are, you won't get anywhere near her. Besides that, she's extremely well-protected."

"How do you know it's a she?"

"I don't. It feels right to call her that." It doesn't make much sense, and I shrug before he brings it to my attention.

"Got it. And what if the baby seems like a boy to me?"

"Call him a he. Believe me, I'll know who you're talking about."

His mouth descends to my stomach. He kisses my baby bump and murmurs something unintelligible against it. Then his smooth, eager mouth kisses a tender trail down to the entrance of my intimate core.

"Oh my *god,*" I groan as his lips brush against the edges of my tender folds.

Mike's ability to reduce me to a twisted knot of over-heated sensation is not new but the intensity of my response even takes me by surprise.

"Stay still," Mike insists.

I can't.

When we were intimate before, our emotional dynamic had been very different. It's fair to say our sexual encounters were motivated by more primitive feelings. Lust, loneliness, and the need to be close to someone without being judged.

The prospect of being parents adds a new dimension to our lovemaking. Instead of primal need driving us, it creates a strong emotional bond between us.

"*Mike....Mike...*" My orgasm robs me of breath. My core pitches and I roll against his face, desperate to maximize the sensation.

He shifts to lie on top of me, his warm flesh slightly sweaty as it presses against mine. His broad tip finds my entrance and lingers there. Inch by cautious inch, he enters me with excruciating tenderness.

He pauses and utters a sigh of relief, his blue gaze capturing mine with hypnotic intensity. This time is different for him, too.

It's the first time we both know it won't be the last time.

He proceeds slowly, exploring me with languid, measured motions, testing the changes in my body and its response to his presence. Mike has changed too. His strokes are more tender, more possessive.

"Jesus *Christ*, Zoe." Mike's early orgasm surprises both of us. He speeds up for a few moments before he stops and collapses on top of me. He strokes my hair and kisses me. After his breathing returns to normal, he rolls off to the side and I bury my forehead against his chest.

Whatever happens now, we know we'll be in each other's lives for a long time.

MIKE

"Oh my god." Zoe gasps from the passenger seat of my car. "What is this place? I thought we were having dinner with your parents."

"We are," I speak slowly and pause. "This is their house."

Zoe's mouth hangs open and an awkward silence fills the car as I maneuver around back and park next to the garage. I switch off the engine when we reach the cobblestone pathway, then we sit in silence together as I wait for her to speak.

"Just how rich are you?" she asks in a quiet, neutral voice.

"Extremely. By anyone's yardstick." I can't hide the truth anymore.

Ever since college, I've done my best to blend in by not calling attention to my family's wealth. I didn't like being hated or judged for it. My nickname "Lucky Mike" comes from those days. To live the way I wanted without revealing too much about my financial status, I won a lot of free pizzas, vacations, raffles, and door prizes.

So yeah, I lied to many people. Why not? I had no more control over the family I was born into than anyone else did. And people lie all the time to protect their privacy. Why should this be any different?

Except now, with impending fatherhood on the horizon, I need to do what I can to help and protect my child. This means having the best possible relationship with Zoe. Besides, I don't want hide to things from her. And that's scary because there are things about me she struggles to accept that I can't change.

"My grandfather started his career in residential real estate before becoming a commercial agent. Toward the end of his career, he invested in some of his own projects. At that point, he'd seen too many people make too much money not to try it."

Zoe nods, distracted as her gaze scopes the house and grounds of my parents' massive lakeside mansion. When the silence turns awkward again, I continue.

"Pappy's gone now, but Dad inherited his business and took it to the next level. Instead of securing space for clients, we constructed our own commercial buildings, which we leased, sold, or operated ourselves, depending on the profit outlook. Market conditions helped a lot. So did working capital."

"Capital?" Zoe asks, turning to face me. "As in DC-squared? Is that you?"

"Yes." I'm puzzled. "How did you know?"

"In Mexico," she says. "The hotel brochure said it

was a joint venture with the Daughtry Capital Development Corporation. That's DC-squared, right?"

"It's a subsidiary company. But it all amounts to the same thing." I take a deep breath before speaking. "So you knew while we were on vacation?"

"Not until the last night." She looks at me for the first time since we arrived. "I realized it was important, but I didn't really understand what 'capital development' meant." Zoe gazes back out the window at my parents' house. "Although I'm starting to get the picture."

Her words make me sigh. "They aren't the enemy, Zo-Zo. They only want to help."

"Help?" she asks her voice sharp. "What do you mean, help?"

"With our baby. Their grandchild."

"What?" she explodes. "You told your parents that I was pregnant? What the hell were you thinking?"

Jesus. "Yeah. What's wrong with that?"

"My mother doesn't even know yet." She clutches her slightly swollen midsection. "Goddamn it, Mike."

I rest my head against the steering wheel and take slow, steady breaths. Even I know better than to make a comment about overly emotional pregnant women, as much as I'd like to call it to her attention.

When I'm calmer, I reach over and gently place my hand on hers, which are laced together over her stomach.

"It never occurred to me that you hadn't told your mother. I'm sorry." I squeeze her gently. "Can I ask why?"

"Because I'm only two-and-a-half months along. I wanted some time to myself to come to terms with all the changes before I had to deal with the fallout from anyone else." Zoe removes one hand from her stomach and bites her nail. Since when does she do that? "Make no mistake, there will be fallout."

"Who else knows? Have you told anyone?"

"Chloe knows. She found the pregnancy test. And some nurses at work. They figured it out pretty fast. But besides them, I've told only you."

"I didn't mean to jump the gun. I only told my parents out of necessity."

"Necessity?" she asks. "Whose necessity?"

"The baby's," I explain. "As my child, he's entitled to financial support from my family's trust. I want to make sure he gets what's coming to him." My thoughts turn to Janet and her recent hostile craziness.

"Family trust?" She swallows hard. "What does that mean?"

"Daughtry Capital is a publicly traded company, but the Daughtry family is the largest shareholder. Those shares are owned by a trust that my family draws income from."

"You mean the baby gets a paycheck?" She's incredulous.

Her description makes me laugh. "Sort of. It's a little more complicated than that, which is why I needed to tell my parents. There are a lot of hoops to jump through."

"Hold on a minute, Mike. I'm not sure I want our child to have all that."

"Why not? It's his. Or hers. They will never have to

worry about food, shelter, clothing or getting a good education. How could you not want that?"

"Because something like that always comes with strings," she replies in a self-assured tone. "Either from the people providing it, or others who know you've received it."

A shudder runs down the back of my neck. She's not wrong. Haven't I struggled with this my entire life? If it's not the sometimes absurd demands of my family, it's people finding out who I am and thinking I've never had a bad day or setback.

"As parents, we have some say in this. That's why we need to have this conversation now." I caress her cheek and turn her face to look at me. "Trust me? Please?"

"I… believe you." She stares straight into my eyes. "I'm just not sure I trust anyone right now. Every minute brings a new revelation."

"I know it must seem like that, but that's because there's a lot to take in, just like you said. No one's trying to deceive you, Zoe. Least of all me."

Zoe smooths the brushed wool of her gray cargo pants, then pulls the hem of her faded long sleeve T-shirt over her expanding waist. Her normally flat stomach has started to swell, exposing a sliver of belly flesh.

"Okay, Mike. Let's get this over with. But that doesn't mean I've agreed to anything. Got it?"

"Got it."

ZOE

MIKE LEADS ME UP THE COBBLESTONE PATH TO THE
front door. His grasp on my hand is relaxed, while his
pace is uncharacteristically slow. He really has been very
sweet, understanding, and gentle. It's all so different
from what I remember about Chloe's dad when Mom
was pregnant. He tried to help and be supportive, but
there was a tense undercurrent that never left.

I'm beginning to relax and accept that things will be
okay.

Before Mike can turn the knob, the door flies open
and a tall, attractive woman with long red hair stands in
our path. She's way too young to be Mike's mother.
Blame it on hormonal irrationality, but she looks like a
bitch.

Sometimes I run across people like her in the ER.
They're hostile, reluctant to give you any information
and resent your questions even if they showed up on
their own. They're usually angry about whatever's

happened, afraid of what's coming next, and resentful of their role.

I tell myself to stop being unfairly judgmental, that this is the result of stress and pregnancy. But if that's true, why is Mike squeezing my hand like a vise?

"What are you doing here, Janet?" Mike asks after they glare at each other.

"I'm here for dinner. Mom said I could stay," she replies with this and-there's-nothing-you-can-do-about-it-sneer.

Mike glances back at me, then adopts his easygoing, situation-diffusing demeanor.

"This is my mistake. I'm sorry, Zoe. We're here on the wrong night." Mike's eyes glisten with anger as he watches Janet. "Let's go."

As we turn to leave, his sister calls out to him.

"No, you're not. This is the right day."

Mike stops in his tracks and turns to look at her. "This has nothing to do with you, Janet."

"That's what you think," she replies with that bitchy sneer.

No doubt about it. She's a real piece of work.

"Good night," an edge creeps into his voice.

Mike turns around and guides me from behind back down the cobblestone path to his car. We're only a few steps away when a second female voice calls out, and it stops Mike in his tracks.

"Michael Gavin? What are you doing?"

Mike's eyes meet mine before he closes his lids shut, pinching the skin above his eyebrows into wrinkles. He opens them, gives me a quick smile and turns back around. His large hand presses on my hip, steering me behind him.

"Mom," he replies. "What is this? Zoe and I were supposed to have dinner with you and Dad."

"Don't be ridiculous," Mike's mom steps off the porch and waves us into the house. "Both you and your sister are welcomed here anytime. You know that."

Mike exhales loudly and exchanges glances with his mother. A moment later he turns around and ushers me toward the door.

"You must be, Zoe." His mother reaches out to me. "I'm Michelle Daughtry, Mike's mother."

"It's nice to meet you." I take her hand and smile.

"Have you met my daughter, Janet?" she asks.

"Not yet." I look past Michelle. "Hello, Janet."

"Hi," Janet answers without smiling.

Michelle clears her throat. "Let's go in. Dad's waiting."

They usher Mike and me in front of them and close the door. It makes me feel like they're trying to prevent our escape.

Michelle and Janet walk behind us, their forced whispers just out of earshot, as Mike ushers me through the entryway down a long narrow hall that reminds me of an airport runway.

It's impossible not to notice the size and scale of this modern Gatsby-esque castle. I've never seen such expensive-looking furnishings. The wallpaper is textured cloth that gives a 3-D effect to the design. The area rugs contain elaborate patterns with a smooth sheen that must be silk. The furniture looks like it belongs in a modern museum of art.

It's lovely and perfect in a tastefully vulgar way. And I can understand how being surrounded by such beautiful expensive things might give someone a sense of comfort and security.

I don't find it relaxing or inviting. The whole place sets me on edge.

"Where are we going?" I ask Mike.

"There's a sitting area next to my father's study. It's where we hang out when we're all together," he explains.

Are we there yet?

I'm about to ask out loud when we turn the corner and find ourselves in what must be the third living room I've passed since arriving.

"Dad?" Mike calls out.

Mike's father sits on an elaborate dark couch that looks like it belongs in a throne room. He points a remote at the massive flat screen television that dominates the wall like it's on the bridge of the *Starship Enterprise*.

"Mike." He greets his son with a clap on the shoulder and a quick hug. "Thanks for coming."

His dad has silver-blond hair and the shape of his nose and cheekbones reminds me of a hawk. He's thinner than his son and not as tall. But those eyes, ice blue chips of flint, are his gift to Mike.

"Come meet Zoe, Dad."

Both men turn toward me where I'm hanging back near the room entrance. Mike's dad is also dressed casually, but it's now I see that even their casual clothes look expensive.

The unique design of the shoes, the subtle patterns weaved into the cloth of his button-down shirt. Even the denim of his jeans has an unusual shimmer.

It reminds me of when I stroked Mike's muscular thigh on the couch at my house and noticed the smooth tight weave of the fabric. I'd never felt denim like that before. I know that's just who they are, but somehow it feels… disingenuous.

"I'm Niles." He extends his hand, then cradles mine in both of his when I do the same.

"It's nice to meet you." I try my best not to sound uncomfortable.

"Michelle?" Niles calls to Mike's mother. "Is dinner ready now, or do we have time to relax?"

"There's time," she says.

"Excellent," he replies. "Please make yourself comfortable, Zoe. And can I get you anything to drink?"

As soon as Niles asks, an awkward hush fills the room. It's a perfectly normal, polite question, but thanks to the reason for my visit, it turns up the awkwardness a few notches.

"Jesus, Dad." Leave it to Janet to make the situation worse.

Niles gives her a puzzled look before his eyes widen. "Oh well, I guess that's a bad question." His laugh is uncomfortable.

"Not at all," I insist. "I'd like a sparkling water if you have it."

"Of course." Niles heads to the wet bar by the fireplace. "When Mike told us the news, we couldn't wait to meet you," he says, handing me a bottle of lemon Pellegrino.

"Speaking of meeting," Michelle says as she sits on the long couch beside me, "how did you and Mike meet?"

"Mom..." Mike warns as he comes to sit on my other side.

"We met in the ER after he was hurt in a fight."

Michelle and Niles exchange worried glances. "Mike was hurt?" Michelle asks.

"In a fight?" his father chimes in.

Beside me, Mike bristles. It's clear his MMA activities are a family sore spot.

"It wasn't serious." I try to smooth things over.

"We jumped the gun a little at the gym," Mike says. "It was just a precaution."

"A *precaution?* My brother? How completely out of character."

Niles' mouth drops open, shocked. My entire body recoils. Mike's hand crushes my thigh. When I look up, a muscle twitches in his cheek as he gives Janet a look filled with fury.

"*Janet,*" Michelle explodes.

"Not that it's any of *your* business," I find myself speaking, "but sometimes precautions fail despite our best intentions."

"So the condom broke?"

"What the hell is wrong with you?" Mike leaps to his feet and approaches his sister, but Niles blocks his path.

"For Christ's sake, Janet," Niles barks at her.

But Janet doesn't hear him. Instead, she's staring at me with a hostile glare I return without wavering.

"I'm an ER nurse, Janet. If you're trying to intimidate me with your unvarnished view of the world, well... Good luck with that." I reach up and grasp Mike's hand a few steps in front of me. "And no, the condom didn't break. It was my hormonal birth control that failed."

"That's convenient."

"Strangely enough, I can't think of anything more inconvenient than an unplanned pregnancy."

Janet gives a snort of disgust and leans over the high-back chair next to the fireplace.

"So this was an accident?" Michelle asks in a sad voice.

"Just like fifty-percent of pregnancies are, yes," I reply.

"I'm not sure that's the right word." Mike jumps in. "We both wanted children. Someday. We just weren't counting on them right now."

And not necessarily with each other.

"Then why are you having one now?" Janet asks.

"Excuse me?" My hostility matches hers.

"Mike's a lot of things, but poor's not one them. What are you? Early twenties, tops? Why the rush?"

I look around at everyone's stricken expression. It's impossible to tell if they aren't speaking because of the shock, or because they're waiting for me to answer.

From across the room, Mike's eyes meet mine. His face is a mixture of shock, fear, and rage. His tortured expression tells me he's no less hurt by his family's behavior than I am. It's been clear since we arrived that they've ambushed him, while their behavior has given me clarity.

At first, Mike's lies about his job, wealth, and our trip to Mexico had upset me. But after meeting his family and enduring their unveiled hostility, along with the obvious blind eye his parents turn at Janet's behavior, it's clear he was trying to distance me from it all.

"I'm twenty-three, Janet. I've got a job with health insurance and a place to live. It's when you don't have those things that people worry about a rush." I give her an assessing look. "But I am curious. What's your hang-up?"

"My what?" she repeats in disbelief.

Clearly, she's not used to getting any back.

"Since we're getting so personal, how old are you? Thirty? Thirty-five? Or have you reached a stage in life where's it's considered impolite to ask?"

"I'm thirty-two." She tells me in a tight-lipped voice.

"Really?" I ask. "And what are you waiting for? Is it some rich people's thing where you want the kids and grandparents drooling and in diapers at the same time?"

And now it's my turn to send shock waves through the room. Michelle Daughtry gasps. Janet looks shocked. But when I look at Mike, his expression softens and his whole body relaxes. He might be reluctant to defend us from his family. But I'm not.

"Zoe, please." Niles distracts me with a gruff voice. "This is getting out of hand."

"With all due respect, Mr. Daughtry, if you wanted to

keep things polite, you should've shut Janet down when she brought up broken condoms."

"She shouldn't have said that." Niles shoots Janet an angry glare. "But there's no point in continuing along this path."

"I agree." I rise from the couch. "Good night."

"Don't go. Please," Michelle asks me from the couch.

I look at a Mike and shake my head. He nods back at me. "We've all had enough for one evening. I'm taking Zoe home. We can try this again another time. Under different circumstances," he adds with a glint of anger in his tone.

"We'll discuss that later." My response lacks enthusiasm. "Take me out of this gilded cage."

"Follow the marble tiles back around to the door," Mike answers. "I'll catch up with you in a few minutes."

"If this going to be a problem, I can call an Uber."

"Don't do that. I'll take you home. Just give me a minute," he pleads.

My gaze locks on Niles. "I didn't how wealthy Mike was until he drove me up to your mausoleum." I turn to Janet "Meeting you makes it easy to understand why Mike wanted to hide the truth. It's no wonder he keeps you at arm's length."

The only audible sound is the click of my heels on the marble floor echoing in the stunned silence.

MIKE

"WHAT THE HELL WAS THAT?" I TURN TO MY FAMILY
when the sound of Zoe's footsteps disappear.

"Michael, calm down," my mother warns me.

"This is *your* fault," I accuse her. "Why on earth
would you invite Janet? This is none of her business.
And for Christ's sake, stop pretending that no one
notices how unhinged her behavior has become."

"Unhinged?" Janet interrupts. "What's unhinged is
you and her having a baby together."

"I don't recall asking for your opinion, let alone your
presence here tonight." She evokes a mixture of disgust
and disappointment. "Zoe's right. We're not children.
The two of us are old enough to make this decision
without anyone's approval, especially yours, Janet."

No wonder Zoe wanted to keep things private. I
didn't expect Janet to be here. Is she saying what my
parents are afraid to tell me themselves?

The thought makes me sad.

Naturally, I expected them to be a little shocked, but I'd really hoped meeting Zoe would put them at ease. She's sweet, accomplished, and level-headed. I could have done a lot worse.

"Mike," my father intervenes, "despite Janice's abrasiveness, she has a point."

"She does?" I reply. "And what point is that?"

"You're going to be a father now. That comes with certain responsibilities."

"I'm aware, Dad."

"You need a steady income and a stable background to raise a child."

"I have those things. So does Zoe."

"You mean your income from Daughtry Capital and your trust fund payments?" Janet chimes in.

The hairs on my neck stand up like porcupine quills. "That's what I mean, Janet."

"Exactly. This MMA stuff is not a real job."

"It is real. I get paid to fight. As for my family income, I'm no less entitled to it than you are. The same goes for my son."

"It's a boy?" My mother can't suppress her curious excitement.

"Oh please," Janet bellows before I can answer Mom. "It's not a welfare program."

I laugh in disbelief. "Really? You think you're being groomed for the CEO position because of your extraordinary management abilities? Or is it those people skills? The only thing you've got going for you is that big silver spoon in your mouth. Same as me. I'm just man enough to admit it."

"Michael!" my dad yells in a rare display of anger. "Don't talk about your sister like that."

"Right, Dad. We can't have reality biting Janet. That's what passes for a family tragedy in this house."

"At least she shows up every day," he complains.

"You *know* why I don't show up every day."

"Because you're too busy working out?" Janet complains.

"Because I think *you* are incompetent." My self-control snaps as I jab a finger at Janet.

The whole room goes silent for the first time since the evening began. Janet glares at me with hostile disbelief, but I stare her down without flinching. When I give her an indifferent shrug, she realizes I'm serious.

"What?" she asks, shocked.

"I think you're an extraordinary CFO who will be a disastrous CEO, in the same vein as McDonald's Harry Sonneborn. Dad's chosen to placate my MMA interests rather than allow a confrontation about it. He seems to think you'll get over it. Or something."

Janet's eyes pool with tears as she exchanges looks with both of our parents. "Is that true?"

"Janet." My mother gets up and walks toward her. "It's been a rough year. We're trying to give you some time. Make adjustments." Mom exchanges a worried look with my dad. "Your father's still around. You'll be fine."

"Is it true?" Janet asks our dad. "Do you agree with him?"

"I haven't decided yet," he admits.

"That's just great." She hugs her midsection. "I'm done. Good night."

"Janet... wait. Please," he calls after her.

Janet says nothing. She gives us a dismissive wave before disappearing down the hall. When she's gone, my dad turns to me, his face a mixture of disappointment and anger.

"Did you have to do that?" he asks.

"Me? This evening was supposed to be about Zoe and our son. Why the hell was Janet here?"

"I'm sorry about that. I really am. But your sister's presence will not change the outcome of the evening."

"What outcome?"

"Mike, the family's been patient long enough. If you want to keep your salary, you need to show up at the office. That's just how it is."

"Patient? There's no coming around on this, Dad. This wasn't about me taking a break from reality. This was about me building a new life for myself. I won't work for Janet, nor will I fight her for control of the company."

"Then work for me, son."

"For how long? Until I've abandoned the life I've built for myself and you hand the reins over to Janet? Is this your way of giving her what she wants while making it my fault to clear your own conscience? I'm sorry Dad, but no."

I glance at my mother, who gives me a familiar scowl. She's not surprised by my decision. At least not as much as my father seems to be.

"Fine. Effective immediately, you won't be drawing

your salary." He folds his arms. "I know you're using your trust fund to build up your own private portfolio. It will take me longer to mess with that money, but I'd advise you to rethink your cash position."

Fuck. I should've seen this coming.

It's crossed my mind, but I kept shutting it out. Janet had expressed her intent to run the company when I was still in college. I'd never wanted to start a family feud over the business. But I'd refused to believe if I didn't fight that my family would shut me out.

Big mistake.

"How pathetic. Janet's bitterness has infected you like a disease. And now you want to punish me, Zoe, and your grandchild. Your only grandchild at the moment."

"This isn't only about Janet. It's about you, too," my dad's impatient, frustrated tone echoes around the room.

"That's bullshit," I reply. "I don't know what's happened to her in the last year or two, or why she and you think I'm to blame for it. But I promise you, Dad, you shut me out and give her the keys to the castle and I'm not the only one who will suffer financially. Or otherwise."

"Mike, do you want to see the company fail?" my mother asks me.

"No. But unlike you, I see that putting Janet in charge puts us closer to that reality. If you don't want me, fine. But then you really should consider someone else. At least until she gets her shit together. And while you're at, stop punishing me for the ways things turned out."

ZOE

"I'm sorry, Zoe," Mike tells me in a somber voice
as we drive toward the city.

"Mike, relax." My calm surprises me. "It wasn't
anything I didn't expect. Although I expected it to come
from your parents rather than your sister. *That* was a
little bizarre."

"Yeah, it was." He blows out a breath. "For about a
year and a half, she's been bitter toward me. And I don't
know why. I've caved into her every demand, and now
I'm screwed, anyway."

While I'm beyond furious with his family, I can't
help feeling sorry for Mike. From the moment we
arrived things had not gone the way he expected. He's
trying to hold it together, but the nasty scene has him
shaken and not just about money.

"You know, my father didn't have a pot to peel pota-
toes in, but it didn't stop anyone from accusing my mom
of having me to trap him. You and your family are super-

loaded. I'm surprised no one asked for a DNA sample."
Self-derision, my weird way of providing comfort.

"I wouldn't put it past them." He grimaces.

I laugh out loud. "Yes, all of us single mothers out
here, setting ourselves up for a life of financial freedom
by giving birth to babies with absentee fathers."

"I don't plan on being an absentee father, Zoe."

"Of course not. But they haven't really put the
screws to you yet, have they?"

He takes a deep breath and I know whatever blowout
happened after I'd walked out hadn't left Mike
unscathed. We drive along in silence, and I try to draw
peace from the distant sound of the water lapping against
the lakeshore.

"My father did," Mike admits with clipped anger.
"He told me that if I didn't quit MMA and go back to
working full time for the company, he'd cut off my
salary and my trust fund income."

"Ouch." Now it's my turn to sigh. I'm not surprised
that something like this happened. "Do you want to work
in the family business?"

"With Janet in charge? And constantly pissed off at
me? Hell no."

"Then don't." My answer is simple.

"How can you talk like that?" Mike vents at me.
"This is serious."

"Mike, you won't ever be the father your baby
deserves or the man I know you want to be if you make
that choice for anyone but yourself. You'll resent me and
your child for giving up the life you wanted. Spare us all
that. Please."

We continue in silence until Mike pulls the car into a public park off Lakeshore Drive. He does a circle before finding a metered parking space, cracking the windows, and switching off the engine.

"That's very noble Zoe, but sort of unrealistic, don't you think? We have a baby coming and I've been cut off from my income sources."

"I would never consider giving birth if I didn't finish school, earn my own income, have health insurance and a place to live. As harsh as it sounds, I wasn't counting on anything from you or your family."

"That *is* harsh." Mike sounds bitter.

"I'm not immune to the things money buys. Do I wish we lived in a nicer house? Or wore better clothes? Had unlimited tuition money? You can bet those perfect pecs and beautiful biceps on it. But I'd rather settle for what's mine, here and now, than risk it all on someone else's whims."

I can't keep the bitterness out of my response.

Does he think I don't like pretty outfits, or getting my hair done at the salon? That I wouldn't prefer to drive a sporty new Mini Cooper instead of sharing a beat-up Toyota with my mother? Sure. But then there's no money to help my mother and sister, or a way for me to go back to school. Perhaps in Mike's world, where he's never had to make such choices, it all seems overwhelming and complicated. But for me…these kinds of trade-offs are no-brainers.

"Do you have any idea what an amazing woman you are?"

His words interrupt my thoughts. When I look over

at him, he's studying me with a look of astonishment mixed with admiration. "You've had to deal with so much, and yet what you've accomplished in such a short period of time is amazing." Mike shakes his head. "I must sound like a real douche to you, sitting here whining about my trust fund."

"No, you don't. You're human, Mike. Of course, you'd freak out when your entire life is upended." I stroke his arm in a soothing manner. "In some ways, it must be worse for you, because you rely on money to solve problems, and that's been taken from you."

"I'm scared shitless. But being with you makes me feel like anything is possible." He leans over and kisses me on the top of my head. "Thank you for that."

"Always remember Mike, that your definition of 'nothing' is what some people work all their lives to get. You have more than you think. Use it."

MIKE

"Looking good, Daughtry." Doug claps me on the shoulder as I exit the cage. "Lean, too. How much have you lost?"

"About fifteen pounds." It's amazing how fast it comes off when life as you know it crumbles all around you. "I gave up alcohol and processed sugar." *And money.*

"How's that working for you?"

"It's kind of a bitch, but I feel different too. I think I can get used to it." Like there's any choice at the moment.

"Yeah, if you want this to work, you will. Most guys give up those things to stay fight ready. Losing ten pounds a week before weigh-in is doable. Much more though..." Doug shakes his head.

"A metaphor for life," I grumble.

"What?"

"Nothing."

True to his word, Dad had cut my company salary off at month's end, about two weeks after that dysfunctional dinner with Zoe. Mercifully, it's a little harder to screw me over with my trust fund. September was the end of the quarter, so I've got that check, but after this, I'm on my own.

That's a problem.

Before that shit-show starring Janet, I'd lived on my DC-squared salary and used the trust fund to invest in my own real estate portfolio. I knew someday, probably after Dad passed, my time at Daughtry Capital would end.

But I'd never expected a screeching halt.

While that check is enormous, it's already spent on property expenses by the time I receive it. October's almost over and the portfolio I've worked hard to build is now available at fire-sale prices.

That includes the mixed-use building which serves as the current home of DeadFall MMA. None of the guys know I own the place, not even Rodgers. There's my apartment and the one next to it that I'd planned to renovate into a single residence. Then there's my Mexican villa, which was a splurge even for someone like me.

I'd paid it for using income generated from larger commercial properties, namely my stakes in the hotel in Punta and St. Rafe's.

St. Rafe's… that's one I'm glad I never told Zoe about. We love it so much, it will break both our hearts to part with that one.

"Hey Doug, you got a minute?" I ask when turns to leave.

"What's up?"

I scope out the gym before I gesture to a quiet spot by the exit. Doug's eyebrows raise a moment, but then he quickly joins me. I glance around a final time before speaking.

"Listen, I'm in need of a little extra cash at the moment." I clear my throat. "Do you know of any way a guy like me could earn some?"

"Daughtry, Daughtry, Daughtry." Doug sighs. "Are you asking me what I think you're asking me?"

"Well, if you think I'm asking about smoker fights, then yeah."

Now it's Doug's turn to cast a cautious glance around the gym. Less satisfied than I, he opens the exit door and pushes me out into the alley.

"You need extra coin? I never figured you for the type."

"We're all the type in the right circumstances."

"True that. You know Rodgers would have our balls stuffed and mounted over the cage door for just talking about this?"

"Hey, I don't want to get maimed in some barroom shit fest. I need to make some money."

"I also train guys at another gym. The owner's new. There's talent there, but not enough. He likes to get his guys some experience and make a little coin, too."

"How much?"

"Two, maybe three grand if you win. Less than half if you don't. Depends on the crowd, the pool, who you're fighting."

"Doesn't sound so bad."

"Mike…these fights are illegal as hell, you understand? Something goes south, nobody knows anything."

"I get it. Can you hook me up?"

He watches me for a few seconds, then nods. "Let me make some calls."

"**A**re you sure this is the place?" I ask while staring out the passenger window of Doug's Toyota Tacoma as he slows and turns onto a narrow street next to an older commercial building.

"I'm sure. It's a low-key venue," he replies.

We inch down the narrow street between the tattered brick exterior and a tall fence laced with three rows of barbed wire on the top. I'm familiar with this area of town, and it's no surprise that a smoker fight would be held here.

The place looks deserted until Doug turns at the end of the alley. Cars are packed in tightly against the building. They're almost impossible to notice because they're parked along a loading ramp that leads underground. In the darkness, it's hard to tell how many cars are there, but they go on as far as I can see.

Doug drives past the loading ramp to the opposite side of the parking lot. There are four handicapped spots, and three of them are occupied. Doug takes the fourth, switches the engine off and hangs a handicapped sticker from his rearview mirror.

"Is that for real?" I ask, nodding at the sticker.

"Yup." He tells me in a matter-of-fact voice. "Blind in my left eye."

"Sorry, man. Didn't know."

"Not many people do. That's how I like it."

"No worries here," I assure him. "There are a few things I keep to myself, too."

We get out of the car, and I pull my bag from the back of the truck. When I look up, Doug is scoping out the place.

"What is it?" I ask.

"Wait a second." Doug nods toward two guys walking across the parking lot.

In the shadow of a broken streetlight, two figures move quickly toward a rust-colored windowless door, about twenty-five yards from the handicapped spaces. They nod at us and keep moving. When they're about ten feet from the entrance, it opens by itself. They hustle in without changing stride, and the door closes behind them as they enter.

"Our turn." Doug nods at the building.

We do the same thing, and when we're inside a fiftyish looking guy greets us. He's about five-foot-four, built like a bull, gray at the temples, ugly as hell with a pushed-in face and a nose that's been broken many times.

"Doug," he says.

"Jerry."

"This is the guy?" Jerry looks me over and we exchange nods.

"That's him. Your guy here?" Doug asks.

"He's here. In the back with Evan."

Doug gives him a quick nod then walks down the narrow, dimly lit corridor with me following close behind.

The building looks like it was a machine shop in an earlier life. Holes in the concrete floor where machinery was bolted down peer out from under the mats and gym equipment that now occupy what was once an industrial shop floor.

As we enter the main section, what I see surprises me. There must be three hundred guys in here if you include the ones lining the catwalk above the large boxing ring in the center.

"We're not fighting in a cage?"

"On the spot adjustments," Doug explains. "More people can see into a ring, more customers, more payout. These aren't sanctioned fights. You've got to take things as you find them."

That isn't good for grapplers.

It's much easier for opponents to avoid takedowns and being pinned because ropes aren't as solid as cage walls. On top of that, the sharp corners of the ring give an advantage to a more offensive style of fighting, while giving grapplers less room to work.

Shit.

I had wanted to take this fight not only for the money but to test out the ground game I've worked so hard to develop over the past nine months. I sigh in annoyance and follow Doug over to the far side of the ring to get a look at my fight opponent.

You've got to be kidding.

The guy's huge, at least six foot four, but young and

gangly. Nineteen, twenty tops. He's one clipper size short of a buzz cut, with angry brown eyes framed inside a boyish face. He looks more like a juvenile delinquent than a trained and focused fighter.

Doug's talking to a tall, slim man with silver-gray hair. I'm vaguely aware that they're discussing fight specifics, but my attention never leaves the kid standing behind him.

"Okay," Doug announces, slapping me on the shoulder. "Mike, this is Evan and Little Ricky."

"Hey." I shake hands with Evan, but Little Ricky's hands stay in his pockets and he gives me a curt nod.

I shrug and let out a laugh of disbelief, withdrawing my hand and ignoring the gangly teenager. That seems to piss him off.

"You fight out of DeadFall?" His voice cuts across Doug and Evan's conversation.

"That's right," I reply, turning my attention back to Doug and Evan.

"You ever spar with MadMan Markovski?" he asks.

"At least twice a week." I lock my eyes on Little Ricky's before shooting him a bored look and pretending to ignore him. Instead of getting pissed that he dissed me, I act like he's not worth my time.

"You win much?"

"More than you, by the looks of things."

"Hey screw you, man," he goads. "You don't know me, you don't—"

"Ricky, shut the hell up!" Evan cuts him off.

"Where d'you find this guy, Evan?" Doug asks. "Get a grip, Little Ricky."

"Don't tell me what to do," Ricky barks at Doug.

"This isn't anger management, kid. Being an asshole and being a tough guy are two different things. When you've been around as long as I have, you can tell the difference straight away." Doug turns to Evan. "Despite your classy venue, it's supposed to be a pro fight. Did you bring it or not? 'Cause right now it doesn't look like you got it done."

"I got it done." Evan grunts. "He's young, and he's a hothead, but he's the real deal, Doug. I swear."

"Great." I sling my bag up onto my shoulder. "If you guys are straight on the money and the rules I need to get ready."

"You sure you don't want to go the ER?" Doug asks as we drive down a dark street after the fight.

"What are they gonna do? Give me an x-ray and tell me my ribs are busted? No shit." I grimace in pain as Doug goes over a pothole in the alley. "Besides, I'm not so sure about my health insurance situation at the moment."

Doug nods thoughtfully. "Did you hear a pop or a crack?"

"No."

"Are you coughing or spitting up blood?"

"No."

"Then you're probably right," he concedes. "But you haven't tried lying down yet. That'll hurt like a bitch."

"I've had cracked ribs before. I know what's coming."

"Then you know the drill. Let them heal. Stay out of the gym for at least three weeks. Light conditioning only. And whatever you do"—Doug takes his eyes off the dark street to look at me—"if Rodgers asks what happened, you slipped in the shower or fell off your girl-friend's roof trying to rescue her cat. Seriously, if he finds out about this, we're both fucked."

"Yeah." I reply with humorless laughter.

Some of us are fucked right now.

I've lost my day job, my trust fund income, and now I can't even train or earn extra money fighting. All the cash I have access to is the three-thousand dollars in my hip pocket from winning this lousy rigged fight. Three grand? I've run up bigger bar tabs in a single night. How do people live like this? Guess I'll find out...

My head strikes the side window with a large thud.

"You okay?" Doug asks.

"Fine."

Doug taps out a thoughtful rhythm on the steering wheel with his thumbs.

"You probably shouldn't stay by yourself tonight. Someone around for you?"

"Don't worry, I'm not." I stare out the window, trying to read the street sign. "Make a right up here. It's the third house down from the corner."

The thought of Zoe waiting up sends a strange shiver of excitement mixed with calm through me.

Doug pulls up in front of Zoe's house, where the porch light is on, just like she'd said when I texted her after the fight. It makes me smile and gives me a sense of place, of belonging, which—despite my family background and real estate holdings—I've never experienced before.

"Let me get the door," Doug insists. "Twisting your upper body will hurt."

Despite Doug's help, a loud grunt of pain erupts from me as I move my feet over the edge of the seat and drop to the sidewalk.

"Easy," he warns me.

I walk in slow measured moves up the path to Zoe's house. When we arrive, Doug knocks and it opens almost instantly.

My god, she's beautiful. That luminous skin appears to glow in the porch light, while the dark hair and eyes make her look like a manga character.

"What happened?" She urges us inside.

ZOE

"I hurt my ribs, Zo-Zo," he tells me before air rushes through his teeth as he bends to kiss me and stops. "Got any ice?"

"Where?" I pull him closer to the hall light and unzip his sweatshirt to inspect his bruised torso. "Here?" I ask, running a gentle hand over the swollen area underneath his armpit where the ribs curl around to his back.

"Yeah." He winces. "There."

"It's probably a costochondral separation. That means the ribs have separated from the sternum at the joint." The man behind Mike says in a matter-of-fact voice. "I'm a nurse."

"So am I. And you can't be sure without an x-ray."

"That's true, but he didn't want to go to the ER."

My hand stills on Mike's body. "Why not?" I ask.

"I'm having health insurance issues at the moment."

We exchange glances, and his insistent eyes tell me all I need to know.

"Was there a pop?" I ask.

"Not when it happened."

"How about now? Try lifting your arm or twisting?" I lean in close and listen to the injured area while Mike tries to move. There's a definite clicking sound. "Did you hear that?" I ask.

"This happens to fighters regularly. But without other symptoms, excessive coughing, spitting up blood, wheezing, tightness in the chest—"

"Do you have any of those, Mike?" I ask.

"No."

"—it's just going to hurt like hell. I didn't want him to be alone, in case he had symptoms during the night."

"Thank you for bringing him here." The thought of Mike lying in pain coughing up blood makes me anxious. "I'm Zoe."

"Doug." He gives me an approving smile. "Have we met before? You look familiar."

"Maybe." My full attention turns to him for a moment. "I work the ER at URMC."

"Ah, that's it," he tells me. "I'm a floater in orthopedics. We've probably exchanged hellos over a mangled body or two. Daughtry, you're in good hands tonight."

"Why do you think I insisted on coming here?" Mike's voice brims with impatience. "Can I have some ice please?" he asks me.

"Of course," I answer. "Have you taken anything tonight?"

"No. I didn't even get a damn shower after the fight."

"Why not?" I ask.

"On that note, I'll say goodnight." Doug gives me a quick nod, then turns to Mike. "Take it slow, Daughtry. And for Christ's sake, get your health insurance sorted out."

As Doug leaves, the windy blackness grabs the door, pulling it closed with a deafening thud.

"Jesus." Doug grumbles in surprise. "Sorry about that," he calls out before his footsteps shuffle down our concrete walkway.

Beside me, Mike lets out a long tired sigh.

"Let's get you in the shower," I tell him. "We've only got one, but it's pretty big. I can clean you up in about five minutes."

"I don't need help." He's stubborn and insistent.

"Yeah, you do. Try washing your hair with one hand. Or rinsing off when it hurts to twist your torso. Believe me, when you finally find a comfortable position, you won't want to get up and take a shower."

I take him by the hand and lead him to our bathroom, but before I usher him inside, Chloe emerges from her room.

"What's going on?" she asks in a sleepy rasp. "Why you'd slam the door?"

"It was an accident. Mike was injured in a fight tonight and he's staying here so I can take care of him."

"Oh, my god. Was it an MMA fight or, like, a street fight?"

"I'm still trying to figure that one out." Mike's annoyance accentuates every word.

I run my hands through his hair. "Take it easy, hon."

"Can I do anything to help?" Chloe asks.

"Yes, please. Go to Mom's room and take the bottle of Diclofenac from her dresser. Then get a glass of water and the acetaminophen from the kitchen and put them on the nightstand in my bedroom. Thanks, hon."

"No problem," she replies, racing off to Mom's bedroom.

"Ice?" Mike asks.

"I'll get that myself. We don't have an automatic icemaker and I want to be sure we have enough for the night."

"Damn. I didn't even think about that."

"Don't worry, I'll figure it out. Mom might have some supplies too. She's got back pain issues."

"I don't want to take your mother's things if she needs them."

"I can pick up more at work. We need to look at getting through tonight." I assure him. "Go to the bathroom get undressed. I'll be there in a second."

Mike gives me an exhausted nod and shuffles down the hall.

I'm a little embarrassed that we're so short on supplies. When Mike called me, he hadn't mentioned his injuries. Instead, he'd asked for my help and wanted to come over. Part of me knows he's trying not to be disruptive, but it would have been better if they'd stopped at a pharmacy.

Thankfully, our ice trays are both full, and there are a few packs of frozen peas in here. For the first time in forever, I'm grateful for Chloe's attempts to cook and even my mother's bad back. Between Mom's medications and Chloe's frozen vegetables, Mike should get through the night okay.

"Hello?" I knock on the door.

"Come in," he answers.

Mike stands in the middle of the bathroom naked. That gold-bronze skin flushes red, and his muscular body is a black and purple patchwork of bruises. As a nurse, I know it gets much worse, but…something about seeing his beautiful body damaged makes it impossible to suppress a shriek.

"Don't worry, Zo-Zo," he says. "It looks worse than it is."

"If you say so." I slide past him to the shower and turn on the faucets. "Here." I hand him the bag of frozen peas. "Your job is to keep this on your ribs. I'll do the rest."

Mike enters the large stall with his back facing the stream of water, holding the frozen peas up under his arm. I remove my sweatshirt and stand at the entrance wearing only a tee and sweat pants. Armed with a few fistfuls of Dial shampoo and body wash from the dispenser, I stand on my toes and wash Mike's hair.

"How come you didn't shower after the fight? Or treat this better before you came here?"

Mike gives a short laugh, then winces in pain. "Damn that hurts. Let's just say we needed to get the hell out of there."

"Why?"

"They were pissed off about having to pay out." He leans back, allowing the water to rinse his hair. "Doug went ballistic. They gave us the money, but it came with an angry vibe, so we left in a hurry."

"Why were they so angry?"

"I wasn't supposed to win." Mike sighs, which makes him cough. "The other guy was a douche. Talented for a kid, but unseasoned and more temper than technique. Because I fight out of DeadFall, they assumed I was a MadMan Markovski-style fighter."

"I don't understand." I rub his shoulders and back as the suds stream off his hair. I add more body wash and scrub his back, upper arms and shoulders while moving downward.

"They thought I was a grappler and would be severely handicapped fighting in a ring, fighting someone twenty pounds heavier. Easy money for them, or so they thought."

"And you weren't?"

"Hell no. I came to DeadFall as a skilled Muay Thai Fighter, with plenty of fights in Thailand. All right, they were in my weight class, which isn't the most competitive. It's only been these last few years I've focused on MMA and developing a ground game."

"Ground game?"

"Wrestling techniques."

Neither of us speak while I pump more body wash from the dispenser and move around to Mike's front. Using a washcloth, I gently scrub his face, neck, pecs and down to his abdomen. I stop at his waist.

"How did... you get hurt?"

"That asshat threw an illegal 12-6 elbow at me when I was on the ground. The referee, and I use the term loosely, didn't call it. Fortunately, I got off an unprotected shot to his jaw at damn near the same time. It fractured his jaw, or at least dislocated it. Thank god, because if he didn't forfeit at that point, I would've."

"Why? If he cheated, you should have won anyway."

"Don't make me laugh, Zo-Zo. It hurts too much." He shifts underneath the shower stream. "This was an unsanctioned fight. The crowd likes excitement. You take the good with the bad."

"It sounds like a glorified brawl."

"No. Yes. Well… Sometimes, maybe."

"Why would you do something like that?"

"Because I need the money."

"Oh my god." I shudder at the brutality.

I spend my days treating people's injuries, many acquired during terrible accidents through no fault of their own. How can human beings deliberately do this to themselves? To each other. "This is all my fault. I'm so sorry, Mike."

"Your fault?"

"I shouldn't have encouraged you to cut financial ties with your family." My stomach churns with guilt. "From the moment I met you, you seemed larger than life. You…had so much of everything. Charm, talent, looks, opportunities. And that was before I knew about your money. I thought to myself, 'how can he *not* succeed at anything he tries?'"

"Come on now, wait a second." He tries to reach for me, but the pain stops him.

"No." I shake my head and lean against the wall outside the shower. "You always had so much, but that meant you had more to lose. It was wrong of me to persuade you to give it up without thinking it through. I was wrong."

Mike gives me a patient half smile, then tucks the frozen peas under his arm and grabs me with the hand on his uninjured side. He pulls me into the shower and under the steamy stream, his lips find mine in a firm, reassuring kiss.

"No, Zoe. You were right."

"How can you say that? You're standing in my shower with a pack of soggy peas, trying to treat your busted ribs. Are you crazy?"

"Maybe... a little. It's not all bad. I'm standing here with you." He pins me against the tile wall with his naked hips. "Being poor sucks. I never doubted that. But like the injury, it's a temporary thing. I'll figure it out. What's different now is the absence of constant family arguments about money and the company. It's like a five hundred pound boulder I didn't know was there is gone."

"I didn't mean to cause a rift between you and your family."

"Don't worry, you didn't. It's been there a while. But now, there's so much less plotting and planning in my daily life. There's no hesitation when I believe I'm right. And if I fuck up, it's on me." He plants a gentle kiss on my lips. "You showed me how to live like that. You taught me it was possible. Thank you."

"You're welcome." My reply is devoid of confidence. "Let's finish you up in here and get to bed."

"Okay." His wicked eyes dance. "Let's do that."

MIKE

OUCH.

I'm struggling after a very uncomfortable night. The ice packs and the pills helped me get me some sleep, but the medicine has worn off and all that remains of the ice is a body-temperature puddle in a plastic bag.

Beside me, Zoe lies fast asleep. Out cold and softly snoring, and one fist curled up by her mouth like a small child. Yet another example of going all in on everything. She snuggles next to me, and in better circumstances, I would welcome that tight little body coiled against mine while we spent a lazy morning together.

But right now, I hurt like hell and I roll my body away in pain. The best thing would be to get up out of bed, but I don't want to disturb Zoe or anyone else in the house. Resigned, I rest my good hand underneath the pillow before I try to drift off again.

Sleep almost catches me but before that happens

there's a rapid knock on the bedroom door followed by a quick whoosh, which causes my eyes to fly wide open.

Audrea Inglot stands in the doorway with a shocked expression.

When our eyes meet, she tries to speak but the words seem to choke her. Then she gives me a forced smile before raising her hands in a half-apology, half-surrender and walking wordlessly away.

Shit.

My aching body lumbers out of bed with slow and measured movements. My sweatshirt rests on the dresser, and I suppress an audible gasp after hitching it up onto the shoulder of my injured side. With Zoe still sound asleep, I go in search of her mother.

It's an awkward situation for both of us, but we can't pretend it didn't happen, and I'm sure as hell not going to hide behind Zoe for the rest of our baby's life. As I move down the hall a weird rapid gurgling sound erupts from the kitchen.

An old-fashioned coffee maker percolates furiously in the kitchen. The sound intensifies as the coffee gets pushed into the glass knob on the top before it stops.

"Would you like some?" Audrea asks from the other side of the counter. She speaks with a slight squeak and doesn't look at me, then reaches inside the cupboard.

"Yes, please. Thank you," I reply.

"Do you want any milk or sugar?" she asks, setting two mugs down between us.

"No. Black please."

Audrea pours the coffee out into a tan ceramic mug

and slides it to me. We take a few sips in silence, and when the quiet becomes awkward, I speak.

"I'm sorry about this morning, Audrea. We… Never meant to startle you."

"It's okay." Her voice is less squeaky. "I shouldn't have barged in like that. Zoe sleeps like a rock."

"That's for sure." Shit. TMI, Daughtry. "My match yesterday ended with a set of injured ribs. Zoe helped me out last night."

"Well, it's good to know Zoe didn't give you those." Audrea points out some bruises on my forearm. She's relaxing a bit. Good.

"Would she do something like that?" My question is half-jest, half-serious.

Audrea laughs. "My Zoe is tenacious, capable, loyal and tireless. She loves being a nurse, and would never harm anyone." Audrea hesitates a moment. "But she can also be uncompromising and unforgiving. Sometimes, it makes you wish she'd just hit you over the head and move on."

Now it's my turn to laugh. "If you're trying to scare me, you're too late. I discovered that about Zo-Zo already."

"You have?" she asks.

"Afraid so." I smile

"Mmm… so are you guys together, together?"

"As in *together*?"

"Exactly."

"Sure. I like to think so, anyway."

"I see." Audrea pauses and takes a long, slow sip of her coffee. "And what does she think, exactly?"

I try to control my expression. The fact is, when Zoe and I are with each other it's natural, effortless, unscripted. We don't agree on everything, but it's never gone so off the rails that we've considered giving up. Not for me, anyway.

"We haven't discussed it too much. Zoe should probably speak for herself."

Audrea releases her coffee cup and folds her hands together on the kitchen counter. She gives me an assessing look, then speaks with quiet firmness. "Mike, you're very smooth. But I'm old."

"I don't know about that." My laugh is casual.

"Zoe didn't have a conventional Cleaveresque, cookie-cutter upbringing. That's mostly my fault, and I accept responsibility." Audrea nods up and down. "It's likely that Zoe's idea of a normal relationship is very different from yours."

"It's possible." My weight shifts against the counter. "But so far it hasn't come up."

"And that's my point. If you're waiting for Zoe to bring it up, or declare she's ready for more, that might not happen." Audrea swallows hard. "And if she decides it's over, you won't get much warning."

"And if I go too fast, she'll shut me out." My eyes meet Audrea's. "We both believe in taking things slow. It doesn't mean we're not serious. Have some faith in us. Please."

Audrea says nothing. Her thumbs tap against each other and her eyes well with tears I can tell she's fighting to keep in check. All I know is that I can't fix whatever's bothering her, and if she loses it in front me, we'll both regret it.

"Audrea, if you don't mind, I need to get the doctor's. My friend agreed to take me. Do you mind if I get ready?"

"Not at all." Her voice is hoarse.

"Thank you for the coffee." I touch her shoulder gently. "And for the conversation."

"I hope we can do it again." She sniffles.

"So do I."

I retreat backward to the doorway, then turn and walk down the hall to Zoe's bedroom.

ZOE

"ZO-ZO? SWEETHEART?"

I feel the entire bed shake. What's going on?

My eyes open with slow-motion awareness. Mike is kneeling beside my bed, shaking me with his good hand.

"Mi-ke?" I force myself awake and take in my surroundings. We're in my bedroom. He'd come over late last night. Right. "What is it? Are you okay? Is something wrong?"

"Shh. Everything's fine," he insists. I'm going to the doctor's this morning. Doug is taking me, and he'll be here soon. I wanted to say goodbye and thank you for everything."

"Wait." I sit up in bed. "Doug doesn't need to do that. I can take you."

"Thanks." Mike strokes my hair with his good hand and smiles. "That's very kind. But you've already done more than enough. You were up half the night checking on me and bringing me fresh ice and gel packs. Besides, I think you should speak with your mom."

"My mom?" I hoped we'd be up and gone before Mom noticed anything amiss. "Have you seen her?"

"Um, yeah." He nods. "Actually, she's seen both of us."

"What?" I ask, sliding my feet onto the floor.

"She came into your room to wake you up." Mike shrugs. "You were asleep. I wasn't."

He lets me digest the words.

Damn.

My whole relationship-status-with-Mike is not something I care to discuss right now, especially with her. I'm not sure how to explain it, and I don't want to push things with him because somebody else feels entitled to an answer.

"Then what?" I ask, cradling my forehead in my hands.

"She seemed…surprised, and then she left. It didn't feel right leaving things that way, or hiding in here until you got up, so I went to find her." Mike shrugs. "We had coffee together."

"You had…coffee, with my mom, after she found us sleeping in my room together." I'm apoplectic. "What on earth did you talk about?"

"The weather, the Cubs, her favorite microbrews… What else?" he replies.

"Are you serious?"

"Um, no." He shoots me a what's-wrong-with-you-look. "We talked about us. About you. She's worried, Zo-Zo."

"About me? Why?"

"I'm not sure. I told her there's nothing to worry about. But I think she needs to hear it from you. Or at least get the chance to see for herself." Mike pins me with a pointed look. "Did you tell her about the baby yet?"

"No."

Mike rolls his eyes. "What's your plan? You going to leave for work one day, pop him out and just bring him home, like a sack of groceries?"

"Nooo!" My outburst fills me with instant regret. "I keep wanting more time, you know? All to myself with the baby. I'm only a few months along. That's not so much to ask, is it?"

"I can't make you do anything. But from where I'm standing, it looks like time's up."

"Nooo," I moan in denial.

"Listen, the last thing you or your mom needs is for her to find out from someone else. As of now, she's the only immediate family from both sides who *doesn't* know."

Before I can reply, Mike's phone buzzes. He pulls it from his pocket and reads the screen. "Doug's outside." He kisses me before standing up next to the bed. "I need to leave."

"Okay."

"Talk to her. Please? And call me later."

I nod.

"Oh, one more thing." Mike digs out a dirty white envelope from his sweatshirt. "Here." He hands me one hundred and twenty dollars. "Is that enough?"

"For what?" I ask.

"Everything. The ice and gel packs, the frozen vegetables, your mom's pills."

"Seriously? You hunted me down at work for leaving you money for the bar tab and hotel bill the night we met. You expect me to take this? No way."

He's about to speak when his phone buzzes again. "I've got to go." He shoves the crumpled bills into my hand and gives me an intense look. "I didn't understand back then. I do now."

He gives me a final kiss before turning away, then shuts the bedroom door with a quiet thud.

"So do I." A tear wells in my eye as I stare at the closed door.

"Hey, Mom." I work up my courage, trying to sound relaxed.

"Good morning, Zoe," Mom greets me from her usual perch at the kitchen counter. "Would you like coffee? Or is that not a good idea right now?"

What did she say?

"I think I'll just take juice this morning."

"I'll get it." She stands and heads to the fridge. "Why don't you go sit down? I'll be right there."

"Sure." While I wait for Mom in the living room, I fidget with the belt of my long fluffy robe, tightening and loosening it with nervous energy.

When Mom joins me on the couch, she looks calm and relaxed but tired, too. She's always been a naturally attractive woman, her statuesque frame and coloring are textbook examples of Polish heritage. Her chin length butter-blonde bob contains striking silver streaks and natural waves. Chloe is a perfect younger version of her.

"Use the coaster," she says, handing me a tall glass. I grab an ancient coaster and place it on the coffee table.

Mom gazes at me with an expectant stare, and I take a long gulp of juice. She sighs, then speaks.

"Mike was here, on the Fourth of July. That was the first time he came to visit, wasn't it?"

"Yeah."

"You've been seeing him for a while then?" She traces the rim of her coffee mug.

"Since early summer. Give or take," I reply.

"Mmm. Does he stay the night a lot when I'm working?"

"Never. Last night was the first time and only because he needed help."

"I see. And why did you help him? Out of the goodness of your heart or because he's important to you?"

"Both, I guess." The question makes me uncomfortable. I like Mike and it gets harder every day to classify things into friend/lover/baby-daddy categories.

Mom nods and says nothing. She takes a sip of coffee and stares out the front window.

"It's safe for me to assume he's the father?"

"What?"

She turns to look at me. "You're pregnant, aren't you?"

It's not a question.

My throat becomes dry and tight. I swallow repeatedly, but it doesn't help. "How, how did you know?" A loud whisper is I can manage at the moment.

"Well, I have had a few kids myself," she explains. "Besides, your appearance doesn't give it away in the early stages. It's the behavior changes."

"How long have you known?" I ask when my voice returns.

"A few weeks."

That makes sense. I've been exhausted and nauseous. Looking back, it probably wasn't that hard to notice the changes.

"Why didn't you say something earlier?" I ask.

"Because I wanted to give you the time and space to tell me yourself. But…"

"But what?"

"Well, between you spending most weekends away and sleeping every spare minute you're home, and now Mike staying the night…it's a little hard to keep it all separate."

She takes another sip of coffee and waits for me to respond.

The only response is the fear I'm forced to confront. Fear of what will happen once my mom discovered the truth. *What will she do when she finds out?* It's played in my head like a broken record from day one.

"You probably can't wait to chew me out and scream…remind me how ironic it is, after all the resentment I've displayed over the years about my fatherless childhood." My sobs are a mixture of fear and tears.

"Don't be ridiculous," my mother chides me in a gentle voice. "I of all people know how pointless that would be. It's a child, not some extravagant purchase that can be returned for a refund." Mom sighs. "And if I know you, you were taking precautions that failed rather than being reckless."

"How did you know?" We've never discussed these things.

"Because you were so determined not to be like me." She swallows hard. "But I also know birth control doesn't always work."

I burst into tears and curl up against her. She puts her free hand around my shoulders. "It was a contraceptive ring. I didn't change it at the right time." My tears free fall. "It was a total shock when I realized what happened."

It's been ages since we've sat like this together. Mom lets me take my time. I cry and wheeze and shift until my self-control returns.

"When your father and I got together, I started taking the pill." She strokes my hair, soothing me like a small child. The amount of comfort it provides is startling. "Gramms was Catholic and they weren't big on contraception. That was one of the many reasons I never told her much about your dad or our relationship."

Her voice is steady as she gazes out the window with a far-off look. It's clear she's recalling a painful memory separated by time and survival. "In my late teens, shortly before I met him, I developed anxiety and a sleep disorder. Gramms also experienced them, so she gave me St. John's Wort."

I gasp and stiffen. "St. John's Wort interferes with birth control pills."

"Tell me about it." My mother hugs me tight. "Nine months later, you came along."

"Oh my god." No one had ever told me any of this, not Mom or Gramms. "What happened?"

"Life sucked, that's what. Your dad was convinced I'd gotten pregnant on purpose. It was only years later I learned about St. John's Wort and figured out what went wrong. Not that it would have mattered to him." My mom's voice resonates with detached bitterness.

"Whatever happened to him?" It's a question I've been afraid to ask for years, but curiosity and maturity prevent me from keeping silent now.

"Shortly after, he showed his true colors. Your dad thought of himself as a player with a gift for the grift. By the time he hit his mid-thirties, his looks and reputation were long gone. As far as I know, you were his only child, and he's drifted from job-to-job, place-to-place. He cut us out of his life a long time ago. Good riddance."

For years, I'd heard about how my father abandoned us. Despite the fact that he'd never attempted to call or visit, I always hoped it wasn't true. Not anymore. He'd treated my mother horribly. I'm ashamed because I must have known, but my mom never complained about him. Not even when I was in full-blown tsunami tirade.

"I'm sorry for all the crap I gave you, Mom." As I lean my cheek against her shoulder, it's my turn to comfort her. "I knew what happened, but no one ever told me the details."

"It's okay. You were young. And angry. You had every right to be." She kisses my forehead. "And some

of that was my fault. I only hoped one day you'd understand that I did my best. However dismal it seemed at
the time."

She sounds relieved, and that feeling floods me with
encouragement.

"What about Gramms? How did she react to all
this?" It doesn't seem complete without knowing.

"Things were tense in the beginning. You and I had
no place else to go, so we stayed here. She wasn't happy
at first, but then you came along…" Mom sighs.
"Gramms was never one to stay angry long, and she was
wise enough to know that having no husband was better
than a god-awful one."

"That sounds like Gramps." We both laugh.

She hesitates for a moment. "Zoe, does Mike know
about the baby yet?"

I stiffen then nod. These kinds of discussions with
her take some adjustment.

"Mmm. And what does he think of all this?"

"He intends to be part of the baby's life. He wants to
be a father, no matter what happens between us. That's
what he says, at least."

"Do you believe him?"

"I want to. But even Chloe's father said he'd stick
around but didn't. And I know with him you really,
really tried."

My mom blinks hard but to no avail. "Clint was a
good man who meant well." A single tear, then another
runs down her cheek. "But he has issues. That's why I
always hoped you'd marry someone stable and kind.

Clint had one, but not the other. It can make all the difference in life." Her voice rings with regret.

"Is that why you wanted it to work out between me and Tim? The doctor?" I offer when she looks confused.

"Yes," she admits. "He seemed so normal, so ready for the next stages in his life."

"Hate to break it to you, Mom, but a college degree and a high-pressure job don't always make someone stable. A lot of times they put all they have into keeping it together at work and then become hell on earth away from the job. A real Jekyll and Hyde going on."

"Mike's not like that, is he?" she asks.

"Not at all. He's not perfect." I try to downplay my true feelings. "He gets impatient and cuts corners some-times. It can be kind of a pain. Still though, he's amaz-ing." That last part slips unintentionally.

"A lot of young men act that way. If they're smart, they learn."

"Oh, he's learning all right."

"So… Is there a future in this, aside from a long-term co-parenting arrangement?" she asks.

Nothing escapes a mom on a mission for information.

"I'm afraid to wish for it." It's the first time I've admitted my fear out loud. "If I really surrender to my feelings and it doesn't work out, I don't think I could cope with that."

"It's hard to tell what's best sometimes. Avoiding a bad thing, or losing something wonderful." Mom sighs with disappointment. "But if you're sure he's a good man, then he's worth the risk."

MIKE

CHRIST.

My wingback chair will never be the same.

It's an art déco classic, leather cushions metal frame. Two large sculpted rectangles bolted onto the sides serve as armrests. But Zoe's got her own ideas about how to use them.

Her feet straddle each of the rectangular arms. Those perfect legs are spread wide, bent at the knees and facing me. Zoe's in complete control as she grinds up and down along my engorged, rock-hard cock. The smooth skin of her firm round ass slides against my groin, stimulating, arousing me even more.

But the biggest turn-on of all? Those eyes.

Liquid coal black, they hold me with hypnotic power, seeing, gauging, calculating my reaction to every stroke and caress, every tightening of that taut body on and around me. None of my reactions go unnoticed. Or unattended.

When I throw my head back against the chair and gasp with guttural grunts, Zoe responds by increasing the incredible friction she's creating along my shaft. Through it all, her expression is priceless. A sultry pout of self-satisfaction.

"Mike…Mike…" she repeats urgently as the speed of her strokes changes again.

I lean forward, supporting the small of her back with one hand, while the other grips her knee. Her strokes quicken before they stop, and her whole body shudders for the second time tonight.

Before her orgasm stops, mine begins. My grip on her loosens, and she laces her fingers around my neck, holding us together. I rub my face against her naked breasts and I thrust in and out, fast then slow, until I'm spent.

My head slams against the armchair, and I stare at the ceiling while trying to catch my breath. After a few moments, I drop my gaze to Zoe. Her legs droop over the arms and she leans to one side in exhaustion.

"This pregnancy sex makes me crazy. Am I wearing you out?" She pants and giggles at the same time.

I give her a sober, assessing stare as I consider my answer.

"What?" she asks with a breathless smile.

"I don't think I've been undressed so fast before. Ever." I stare at our discarded clothes, scattered across the floor between here and the front door. "I'm stunned and impressed."

Zoe throws her head back and laughs. We're both

sweating. My ears are ringing, and that infectious sound prevents me from feeling anything but happy.

"Where are you going?" I ask when she attempts to climb off me.

"It's a little cold now." She looks at her clothes on the floor. "Thought I'd get dressed."

"Nope, that doesn't work." I scoot down to the end of the chair scrunch her body against mine as her legs wrap around my waist. "I like you naked."

"Don't drop me," she warns.

"Don't worry." I stand up and grip the bottom of her ass. She squeals, then settles against me as I head to my bedroom.

I carry her through the open kitchen, past the living room to the master bedroom. My intention was to start in here but we never got this far. At first, Zoe had been excited about coming to my apartment, and by the time we had reached the front door she was just plain excited. My shirt was almost off before we made it inside.

"Ready?" I ask before throwing her gently on my king-sized bed and collapsing next to her.

Naked and flat on her back, she peels the large comforter down while she looks around. My room is well-furnished with high-end items. I wouldn't live anyplace that wasn't—at least in my previous tax bracket. And yet it's never really felt like home to me.

"This is an amazing place," Zoe comments as her eyes trace the floor-to-ceiling windows with killer views of the city skyline.

"Thanks."

"How come you never brought me here before?"

"I didn't want you to get the wrong idea."

"What idea?"

"That I'm rich."

"But you are."

"Not anymore. And as I recall you didn't like that about me or any man when we first got together. You assumed I'd treat you a certain way and wanted nothing to do with it. Remember?"

"Mmm. You have been a pleasant surprise. In more ways than one, but…why have you brought me now?"

"Truth? I can't afford St. Rafe's anymore. No, no, don't do that," I tell her when face contorts into a panicked expression. "The other reason is that I wanted to bring you here to enjoy it with me while I still had it." My throat works hard to swallow. "I've sold it."

"You did?"

"Yeah. It sold quick, and for a great price. It's a huge stroke of luck. I might even make a profit and shore up some of my other investments, instead of losing everything like I thought." My mind races at the possibilities. "I'll take more fights to increase my income, but it won't ever be DC-squared money." I blow out a calming breath.

"Oh god, Mike." She strokes my arm. "This is your home."

"Not really." I sigh. "It's always been more of an investment. When it became clear that I would one day part ways with DC-squared, I started to build my own portfolio. Was doing a hell of a job until the money stopped rolling in five years too soon. Still though…" I look around my palatial apartment. "I will miss it."

"And you're okay with letting go of all this?"

"Working on it," I admit.

"Fuck. This is all my fault." Zoe rubs her temples.

"No. Hell, no." I turn to face her. "This is all Janet. You were just the excuse. My mistake was believing my dad would never allow it. You didn't fuck this up. I did." It's a bitter pill to swallow.

"Have you talked to your parents?"

"My dad left a message a few days ago. Probably wants to ask about Christmas. I didn't respond."

"He's still your dad, Mike."

"It doesn't feel like it." My voice is bitter.

"You have no idea. Don't say that," she warns me.

"Sorry, Zo-Zo." I kiss her shoulder.

We lie together, naked, in silence for ages with our fingers intertwined.

"I usually spend Christmas with my family." I'm stunned to hear myself speak. "But lately, I don't feel wanted there, and that sucks this time of year."

"Well…you can come to my house, if you'd like." Zoe's voice is hesitant. "But it's boring, normal people's stuff."

"What is 'boring, normal people's stuff?'" I ask.

"You know…stuff. We'll cook at home, sit around and talk, and watch old Christmas movies. No celebrity chefs will prepare our food, and Adele isn't performing a private holiday concert. Oh, and there won't be any fireworks show on the front lawn. Think you can handle that?"

I laugh out loud. She really has me down. "I would love it. Thank you."

ZOE

"CAN YOU SEE OKAY, MOM? HOW ABOUT YOU, CHLOE?"

"We're good. You're the shortest. How about you?" Chloe asks.

"This seat is fine," I reply. "I'll lean into the aisle if someone tall sits in front of me."

Once Mom and Chloe enter the row, I take my seat on the end. I have a clear view of the octagon from here. Truth to tell, I'm clueless about MMA. I've never even watched it on television before, let alone attended a live match. But it's such an important milestone for Mike that I couldn't miss it.

Mike has invited us to his first major fight as a light heavyweight. His rib injuries have healed, he's super fit, committed and focused. Mike's considered the underdog in this match, something he's tried to ignore.

Months ago, when I had asked him what he wanted for Christmas, he told me, "I want to win my fight. And for you to be there when I do."

"Why do you think you'll win when everyone else thinks you can't?"

"Because they've never seen me at this weight before. And I want it more than him."

"Well, then I don't need a present."

"Why?"

"Because you winning will be my present."

"Merry Christmas," he had promised me.

Tonight, we're both here to collect.

The memory of Mike spending Christmas with me and my family makes me smile, even after so many months. I had never expected to ask him, but when it happened, I had been nervous for weeks. Our backgrounds are so different I wasn't sure what he'd think. The fear he wouldn't find it us good enough, or me good enough, stayed with me.

That fear made me realize I'd fallen in love with the father of my baby.

I learned long ago that my family background couldn't be changed and to move on quickly from people who held it against me. Mike was the first man I've ever been close to whose opinion of me mattered, and I kept waiting for him to decide I wasn't good enough.

Only it never happened.

He hadn't been sure what to expect at our house, but I think that made it fun for him. Christmas is a big deal with the Inglot women, and we take great pride in our holiday preparations.

Mom, Chloe and I had worked for days making our traditional Christmas Eve meal. Since we're of Polish descent, this is when our major celebration takes place.

Dinner lasts all night and consists of wild mushroom soup, pierogies, herring with root vegetables, sauerkraut, and for dessert, Kutia.

No one in my family cooks regularly or well, but we make a wonderful holiday dinner. Mike enjoyed it, which no doubt surprised him after eating some of Chloe's other meals. But the most important thing was the collective realization we all got along.

It had been after two in the morning when we stood to collect the dishes. Aside from throwing his takeout box away, Mike can probably count one hand how many times he's done dishes. But he'd helped, too. After we finished, he'd gathered his coat to leave, but my mother stopped him.

"Where are you going?" she had asked him.

"To my apartment."

"You should spend the night," she told him. "Nobody should be alone on Christmas."

"Thank you, Audrea," he'd replied, touched by the invitation.

"Good night," she told us. "Merry Christmas."

He had stayed the night in my room, his arms wrapped tightly around me. The next morning we got up late, watched *A Christmas Story* and had a snowball fight.

My best Christmas. Ever.

"Excuse us, please," a young man waving two tickets at our row asks me.

"Sure." I stand and let them by.

My gaze follows them to the unoccupied seats next to Chloe with sad disappointment. I'd hoped Mike's family, at least his parents, would show. On top of all their other issues, they were mad he hadn't turned up for Christmas. When I told Mike to invite them anyway, he'd warned me not to get my hopes up.

As the young men take their seats by Chloe, I realize he was right.

"Ladies and gentlemen, live from United Center in Chicago... our next matchup is in the Light-Heavyweight Division. This is a three round match between two contenders."

"Is that him?" Mom leans in and asks me.

"I think so." I crane my neck into the cage to see the men standing in the center. Mike's back is to me, but I recognize his shoulders and the colored trunks. "Yes."

"Fighting out of DeadFall MMA at a weight of two hundred and three pounds, with a record of seven wins and five losses in the heavyweight division, Chicago's own 'Lucky' Mike Daughtry."

Mike nods and waves to the cheering crowd. He stands there wearing only trunks and I'm stunned by his dramatic physical transformation. He's super lean, and every muscular ridge looks etched into his body. I know from...touching him that those muscles have gone from firm and dense to granite-like in their consistency.

My happy-go-lucky, easy going charmer looks relaxed. He remains quiet and detached while the MC introduces his opponent. Nothing about his demeanor gives any indication of what comes next.

The round starts and Mike charges his opponent, landing several hits to the upper body. The other fighter lunges back, but Mike pummels him in the head with fast, *fast* punches. He deflects most of them, but some of them connect.

"And Daughtry lands an early right hook on Ferber!" one commentator announces.

No Shit. Ouch.

I'm no expert, but Mike won't let the other guy fight. Every time the guy tries to square himself for an attack, Mike gives him a fistful in the face. The opponent keeps a defensive posture, but he's unable to launch a successful counter-attack.

"Daughtry's got him backing up. Ferber can't do anything but retreat right now."

As the round continues, Mike's demeanor transforms into something alien. The casual ease evaporates, and he strikes with unrelenting, feral fierceness. Ferber hits him hard in the shoulder and neck multiple times. Those strikes must hurt, but Mike's unfazed. The thought makes me bristle.

"Ferber needs to slow this down or it will be over very quickly."

Mike holds Ferber's neck and shoulders while his knee strikes his face repeatedly. When Ferber tries to grab that powerful knee and upend him, Mike switches back to hand strikes.

When he finally breaks Mike's grip, he finds himself inches from the cage wall. Mike pushes him against it with a simple, vicious shove, then grabs Ferber's legs and pulls them out from under him.

"Ferber's down! He's down against the side of the cage!"

He lies against the metal cage while Mike straddles

his lower torso. With his legs neutralized, Mike pounds the crap out Ferber's head and face. Blood splatters, but Mike doesn't stop. When Ferber can't protect himself from those vicious strikes, his body goes limp, and the referee pulls Mike off him.

"Daughtry has done it! This fight is over by TKO!"

Mike's fast, aggressive tactics earn him a win in the first round. Not bad, especially for an underdog. He runs circles in the ring, waving to the cheering crowd.

Mike raises his fists, and they cheer even louder.

I shift uncomfortably in my chair, then casually look around at the other spectators. While men occupy the majority of the premium seats, there's a good number of women in here, too. Clapping, laughing, whispering… are they as turned on watching Mike as I am?

Our smoldering chemistry and visceral attraction are so strong and obvious to us we've never felt the need to speak about it. But this warrior-god side of him makes me hotter than the hinges on Hell's gate.

For one eternal moment, life treats us to a brief but perfect interlude. He's happy, I'm so delighted and proud of him, and my family is here to share it.

That's when my nightmare starts.

Mike points to where we're sitting from the octagon. As I stand to cheer and wave at him, a warm rush of liquid gushes from between my legs. It feels like I've just peed my pants, but that's not what happened. A wave confusion passes through me as my gaze descends past my now-bulging baby bump.

When I can't see my shoes, I lift my foot. Streaks of bright red blood stain my gray leather boots.

Oh. My. God.

"Mom!" I shout over the cheering crowd. "I need help. Get me to the hospital."

"Zoe, Zoe, calm down. It's okay." Macy MacTaggert soothes me, while she touches the top of my naked knees.

Macy's made short work of my tweed pants with her trauma sheers. She's cut the side of my panties at the hips, moving quickly while giving me as much time as she can to prepare myself.

One gush. That was all.

As opposed to continual, non-stop oozing.

That's a good thing, right?

I try to force myself to be calm and remember my training, but it's so hard to think as waves of panic wash through me.

My baby. Mike's baby. Please let our baby be okay.

"Zoe…you need to spread your legs so I can take these off."

"Nooo, please." The thought terrifies me. It's irrational, but still there.

"Only for a sec. Then I'll get you under a drape. We've called OB/GYN and someone should be here. Like now."

I nod. There's no other way.

"Good. Take a few deep breaths."

I do what she says. On the second exhale, she parts

my knees gently and removes all my clothing. Then she throws a drape over my bent knees.

"You okay?" she asks.

"Yeah. Thanks."

Before she can say anything else, the OB/GYN rushes into the room, and I mutter a silent prayer of thanks. He's a good doc. I nod hello at him through my tears.

"Hey, Zoe." Peter Osmond's greeting is calm and gentle. "How you holding up?"

"You tell me," my worried, tired voice rasps.

"I'll do my best. We need an ultrasound." He looks over at Macy, who's standing by the equipment. "We'll start with an abdominal, but if that's not definitive we'll also do a transvaginal. You ready?" he asks and motions to Macy.

She's already rolled the machine into place by my bed.

Please let our baby be okay.

MIKE

"I'M LOOKING FOR ZOE INGLOT? CAN YOU HELP ME?" I
ask after rushing to the ER admittance desk.

"Do I know you?" A nurse with maroon glasses and
long cornrows studies my face.

"I don't think so." *Why does that matter?* "Can you
please help me find Zoe Inglot?"

"She's not working today." The nurse looks me over.

"No. She's not." I'm getting impatient. "Her sister
texted me about forty minutes ago that they admitted her
to the ER. Am I in the right place?" I twist my neck
around in search of signage.

Her head snaps back. "Zoe was admitted?" she asks
the other nurses.

"Yeah. Macy's with her," another nurse at the desk
replies. "They were waiting for OB/GYN."

"Sorry, I just got here," the nurse with maroon
glasses apologizes. "And you are?"

"Mike Daughtry."

"Are you a relative?"

"No. She's my other half. We're together."

"Not married?"

"No."

"Do you live together?"

"Not yet." *You need a home for that.*

She responds with a slight grimace. "Please take a seat. I'll come find you when I know something."

"The baby's mine," I blurt out. "Is my child okay?"

"I thought you looked familiar." The nurse blows out a breath. "Have a seat. Please? Let me go see what's happening. There's nothing for me to tell you right now. Okay? I promise." Her voice is calm, her expression sympathetic.

"Okay." I retreat to the waiting room.

Have a seat? Now? You've got to be kidding. I pace around a cluster of empty chairs near the back.

An hour ago, I was on top of the world. The biggest fight of my career was done and won. Before it had started, I double-checked to make sure Zoe and her family had arrived and found their seats. Zoe saw it all. Hers was the first face I looked for after it was over.

Winner by TKO.

When I'd seen her last, she was speaking to Audrea. By the time the post-fight remarks were done, they'd gone. It hadn't worried me then. They'd probably gone to the locker rooms to wait for me.

Zoe never showed.

Okay, she'd probably gone to the bathroom. Maybe there was a line. Fair enough. I'd showered, then gotten dressed.

Still no Zoe.

Now I was irritated, even worried. That's when I'd grabbed my phone and saw a text message from Chloe.

Zoe's not well. We took her to the ER at URMC. Come when you can…

Doug had raced me here in record time.

I should have never taken that damn shower.

Why didn't I check my phone first?

A dark, deadened pain engulfs me. Despite our passionate connection and our impending parenthood, we've both been slow and cautious about our relationship. At the end of the day, rich or poor, boy or girl, we all want to be loved for who we are.

Not for money, or guilt, or even nobly convenient co-parenting arrangements. Maybe it's selfish, to expect control over the surrender of that piece of your soul. Many people have no say in the matter.

I never wanted to give it up for less than the real deal. And from the word go, I sensed the same desire in Zoe. Whatever her reasons for being with me, they sure as hell weren't material. Our relationship is crazy, unconventional, even erotic, but it has never been transactional.

When I think about all we've been through, all that's yet to come, and then picture life without her… I *can't*.

Please let everything be okay.

"Mr. Daughtry?" the nurse calls me. "This way."

I race up the aisle, through the double doors, and follow the nurse who's already moving down the hall, past the exam area.

"Where are we going?"

We stop by the elevator doors where she presses the call button. "Zoe was admitted by OB/GYN," she tells me with measured reserve. "The rest of her family should be up in that department's waiting area."

"Admitted? What's happened to her?"

She lowers her voice an octave. "There's not much more I can say. You're not family or a domestic partner." She sighs. "Her relatives can fill you in further."

The door opens, and she touches my forearm. "Good luck to you both."

∾

"Audrea? Chloe? What happening?" I ask when I find the waiting area.

"Mike!" Chloe leaps from the chair and wraps her arms around my neck. "I'm so glad you're here!"

Over Chloe's shoulder, I study Audrea's haunted expression. She acknowledges my presence with a faint nod before she resumes gazing out into nothingness. Her normally smooth hair is messy and I watch as she runs her hand through it, then twists it tightly and pulls hard on the ends.

"Hang in there, kid." I return Chloe's hug with one of my own. Then I walk toward Audrea's chair and crouch down in her line of sight.

"Hey. Audrea? How are you holding up?"

"Like shit." She breaks her gaze with outer space to look at me. "I can't believe this is happening."

"What is?"

"They're doing an emergency C-section." She gulps after the last word.

"Holy Christ." My brain screams while I try to remain calm. "What happened?"

"We don't know." She rubs the sides of her temples. "Zoe started bleeding at the fight. She asked us to take her to the hospital. Thank god there was an ambulance there. EMS got here in five minutes." Audrea cries as she relives the ordeal.

"Hey, hey," I soothe her in a confident voice. "Zoe'll get through this. We all will."

I sit down next to her, throw my arm around her shoulders and try to ignore the racing of my heart. Chloe sits next to her mother and leans her cheek against Audrea's shoulders. Poor kid looks terrorized.

We sit there in silence for what seems like an eternity when a doctor enters the patient family room.

"Uh, Ms. Inglot?" he asks.

"Yes?" Audrea rises to speak to him.

"I'm Dr. Osborne. We met in the ER?"

"I remember. How's my daughter?"

"We've stabilized her. She lost a great deal of blood and required two transfusions."

"Oh Good Lord," Audrea gasps. "What happened?"

"Your daughter had what's known as a placenta abruption. That occurs when the placenta detaches from the uterus before the birth of the child. I diagnosed her in the ER and we rushed her into surgery."

"How is the baby?" I blurt.

"This is…Zoe's boyfriend," Audrea explains.

Boyfriend? God that sounds pathetic and childish,

especially in these circumstances. Right at that moment, something inside me decides that has to change.

"Mike Daughtry." I extend my hand. "I'm the baby's father."

"Congratulations. You have a beautiful boy." The doctor clears his throat. "I'm sure you're aware that your son was right around thirty-four weeks, so he's premature." The doctor gives us time to process that. "He was not breathing on his own when we delivered him, but we got him going within minutes. He's in the NICU, and his doctor there can update you on his condition."

"What's NICU?" Chloe asks.

"Neo-natal intensive care," the doctor answers.

"Will he be okay?" I ask.

"The NIC folks are in a better position to discuss that. This all appears to have happened quickly. The baby was born at a good weight for his age, which suggests he hasn't been under duress for long. From the time Zoe got into the ambulance, to her arrival at the ER, to start of surgery was twenty minutes, tops. I had your son out in less than two minutes." He blows out a breath. "That's about as good as it gets."

"Thank you," I tell him.

"What caused all this?" Audrea asks in a ragged voice.

"We don't know," he says. "We're running tests now. But in some of these cases, we don't arrive at a definitive answer."

"Can we see her?" Audrea asks.

"Soon. The nurses are getting her settled in a room.

They'll come get you. But remember, she will be weak. Try not to tire her out."

"We won't," I promise. "What about my son? When can I see him?"

"Ask at the nursing station. They can check for you."

"Thank you," Audrea tells him.

"You're welcome. Zoe is very well liked and we're all thinking of her."

"Thank you," I reply.

The doctor gives us a quick nod, then turns to leave.

ZOE

I STRAIN TO HEAR THE CONVERSATION IN THE HALLWAY.

Damn it, they're too far away and they're trying to be quiet. *Come closer, please.*

I'm weak and tired from the surgery, so much that the strain of listening and speaking is more than I handle at the moment. Helpless, I lie in the dark hoping and waiting for someone to come tell me all that's happened.

After an eternity, I get my wish. The familiar sound of quick, confident footsteps approaches the bedside of my dimly lit hospital room. A warm, calloused hand reaches for mine. Moments later, his lips brush my forehead.

"Hey Zo-Zo." His voice is tender and gentle as he whispers near in my ear.

At last. "Mike."

"How do you feel?" he asks.

"Tired."

"Then you should sleep," he tells me.

"What time is it?"

He looks at his watch. "About ten in the morning."

"When did you get here?"

"I never left."

I run my fingertips over his razor stubble. "You should rest, too."

"You first," he replies.

"How's the baby?" I ask.

"The baby is fine. He's a he."

"Sweet."

"Are you sure?" he hesitates.

"How could say that?"

"Well…you seemed so intent on it being a girl. I hope you're not disappointed."

I'm fighting sleep, but I don't want him to worry, especially about this. "Mike, the most beautiful thing anyone ever said is 'the baby is fine.' "

"Good." He exhales, relieved. "A girl would've been great, but I'm thrilled with a son."

"Mmm," I whisper. "Tired now."

"Then sleep," he tells me.

"Don't leave yet."

"Don't worry. I've always loved to watch you sleep."

"And I love sleeping with you."

"Soon," he promises.

I feel my lips curl into a smile. Mike takes my arm in both his hands. He strokes my arm with one hand while the other massages my fingers. I'm nearly asleep when I hear a startled gasp from the doorway.

"Mike?"

A familiar voice I struggle to recognize calls his

name. It doesn't help that the room is dark, and it's hard for me to keep my eyes open.

"Hey, what you doing here?" Mike replies.

"Funny, I planned to ask you the same thing." Her footsteps come closer. "I take it the two of you know each other?"

"We do." Mike's words are simple, but his tone speaks volumes. "In fact, we're very close."

The stillness in the room is deafening.

"Is the baby yours?" she asks.

"Yes. And I'm beyond happy about that," Mike insists.

"Jesus Christ, Mike. Why the hell didn't you tell us?" Her tone conveys surprised anger.

Sometimes hospitals suck. There are lots of people around, a lot of things going on, and a lot of moving parts. It's hard to keep all of it straight when you're lucid, but when you've weak, tired and on drugs it's scary and disorientating.

Who is that?

"It's not exactly a secret. We've just had a lot on our plates."

"Do your parents know?" She sounds shocked.

"Yes. So does her mom and both of our sisters."

"Damn. I didn't realize you knew each other. When did you guys meet?" she asks.

"In the ER after my sparring accident. Then again, a few months later at your party for Paul."

Macy? Macy MacTaggert? How do they know each other?

"You were at the party?" She gasps. "*That* night? I didn't see you there."

"We didn't stay."

Another hushed stillness fills the room, speaking volumes.

I can't stand it anymore. I want to keep my work and private life separate. Who I tell at work is up to me. A stress-fueled adrenaline rush gives me the focused energy to overcome my diminished state. For a moment, anyway.

"Macy? Mike? Why are you telling her all this? It's none of her business."

"Easy, Zo-Zo," he tries to soothe me. "This is my cousin's wife. We're not only related, we've been friends since middle school. She's not your nurse."

"He's right, Zoe. I was on my way out and wanted to check on you. I never intended to be intrusive." Macy's voice is soothing, but changes as she continues. "Although, I didn't expect to run into any of *my* family members up here. Congratulations to both of you."

Without another word, she exits the room.

"Why didn't you tell me?" I ask in a sleepy voice.

"Truth?" he hesitates.

"Always!" Damn, my temples pulse.

"When you and I first got together, Macy would mention you sometimes. It was no big deal. It's not like her chattiness is confined to one subject or person. But I enjoyed hearing the occasional story, so I never told her about us. Besides, you worked with her, and it didn't feel right to mess with that."

"You weren't... ashamed of me?"

"Ashamed of you?" he repeats. "What the fuck are talking about? Never. I assumed she'd find out either from you or the family once my parents were told."

"Promise?" The throbbing of my temples slows down.

"Promise."

"Good." It's the only thing I can say before sleep overtakes me.

MIKE

Talk about a reversal of fortune.

A short time ago, I was a high-income earner with a spectacular personal real estate portfolio. Now I don't even have a place for Zoe and our baby to stay together. How fucked is that?

Dejected, I shut the hospital room door and step into the hallway in search of Chloe and Audrea. But before my search starts, it's interrupted by a tall, familiar figure walking down the hall toward me with a concerned look on his face.

"Michael?"

"Dad? What's going on? What are you doing here?"

"I came to see... How you were. Macy called and told me that you were here with Zoe."

"Macy should mind her own business." My reply is stern.

"Well, blame me and not her." My Dad is just as stern. "I asked them to tell me if they heard from you.

You didn't come for Christmas and you never call me back."

"And this surprises you? After that nightmare family dinner, you treated us to at the house?"

My father exhales in his familiar way. Since I was a child, it's been his way of communicating irritation and a warning that he's attempting to control his temper. "I tried to apologize. Had you returned my phone calls, you would've known that. As for the rest, you quit your job, Mike. That's not my fault."

"I, I…quit my job?" I stammer. "Is that the latest version of events? Don't hold out for me to agree with you, Dad. I didn't quit my job. I agreed not to start a family feud. When that threat faded into the background, Janet forced me out. And you let her do it."

"We need to talk about this."

"No Dad, we really don't." I try to walk past him, but he touches my forearm.

"Please." He nods toward the stairwell. "Just take a few minutes."

I don't know why, but I let him steer me through the stairwell door, where we stand on opposite sides of the doorjamb and face each other.

"What is it?"

"It's your sister. She's suffering." His face is haunted with worry.

"Well, she's not the only one. Janet's made everyone else that way with her vindictiveness. At this moment in my life, Janet's issues are the least of my concerns."

"You don't understand, Mike. She endured…some kind of…trauma, about a year and a half ago." Dad rubs the back of his neck. This is a difficult discussion for him.

"What happened?" I ask.

"We don't know. She won't discuss it. Your mother and I think whatever happened, Janet thought she could get through it on her own, but trying to tough it out alone only made things worse."

The hits just keep on coming. Fuck, I'd rather be beaten senseless in the ring. At least you can meet it head on and understand what it's about.

"I'm madder than hell at her. But I don't wish her harm. She's my sister."

"I know, son."

"Is there something I can do?"

My dad gives a tormented, puzzled look before he speaks. "You know, she's especially angry at you."

"So it's not just my imagination? That's a relief."

"Do you know why? Did you have a falling out over something your mother and I don't know about?" His voice is tortured.

My mind races back eighteen months. "No, no. She didn't like the Mexican resort deal. We went back and forth about it. A lot. Janet even took a team and went down there for a month. But it worked out well. Very well, for everyone. I have no idea why she was mad or still would be."

My father's laces his fingers behind his neck and looks up at the stairwell. "Well, this has gone on long enough. I'm no longer convinced we're helping my daughter, and I refuse to alienate my son anymore."

"That's great to hear. Really. I've missed you and

Mom, too. But right now is not a good time. I've got to focus on Zoe and my son."

"How are they?" he asks with genuine concern in his expression.

"The baby's in the Neonatal ICU. They expect him to be out in a few days. But Zoe… She lost a lot of blood." My voice cracks. "She needed two transfusions."

"Good god." He rests his hand on my shoulder. "I'm so sorry, Mike."

I grip my father in an embrace. "Thanks, Dad. The docs are optimistic, but she's weak, and will be like that awhile."

"Where are the two of you living?"

I grunt in disgust. "I'm homeless. Or rather, property-less at the moment. I'm staying at St. Rafe's, but Zoe doesn't want to live there with a newborn. She'll go back to her mom's until I get something sorted out."

My dad nods as he takes in my words. "I've got a proposition for you, Mike. One that might make things better for everyone."

"What is it?" I can't help being suspicious.

"Come back to the company, and I'll support you for the CEO position with the board."

"Dad, please…" I back away for him.

"Listen, Michael, I've still got enough clout to pull it off. But you've got to hurry," he pleads. "I'm sorry to push right now, especially at a time like this, but we have a limited window of opportunity."

"Dad, nothing's changed."

"You're wrong. Before, I refused to side with one of

my children against the other." He stares off into space, then looks me in the eye. "That's changed."

"How?"

"Janet's explosive behavior has spilled over into her work life. There are complaints about how difficult she's become, and a few key people have quietly approached me about leaving."

"So now there're ramifications at the company? I warned you."

"You did. And to be honest, at the time I found it self-serving." He takes a deep breath. "You wanted to keep your salary and still avoid Janet. I am sorry."

I sigh and lean my head against the gray cinderblock wall next to the stair door. "If I end up in a showdown with Janet, things could get ugly."

"They might." My father's worried expression returns. "Lord knows I've done my damndest to keep you two from each other's throats. But you're grown now. And I'm old. The time I have left…" He turns to face me, "… I want to spend with your mother. And my grandson if that's possible."

"Wait a second." A wave of fear rushes through me. "The time you have left? What the hell are you talking about?"

My Dad folds his arms. He looks weak, tired and resigned. "I'm ill, Michael." The words echo off the stone walls of the stairwell.

"What?" I can barely hear my voice. "What is it? What's wrong?'

"Leukemia." His voice is matter-of-fact. "I. Have. Leukemia."

This can't be true. Not *my* dad. He's always been so strong, tough, and energetic. True, he's spent his life obsessed with the company, but he's always been present, too.

This can't happen. Not now. First Zoe, then Dad?

"Oh no. No, Dad."

"I've started treatment. It's going well, but… I just can't keep pace at the office anymore. If I'm honest, I don't want to. For the last forty-five years, I've put my heart and soul into this company, and it has been very, very good to me. To the entire family. I've had a hell of a run, but I'm done now. Time to move on."

I fall to my knees against the wall and blow out a long slow breath. There's too much going on right now for me think it through. But it doesn't change the fact I need to do something. Soon.

"If—*if* I agree to your offer, what's the timeline?"

My dad rubs the back of his neck and slides down the wall and kneels next to me. "Zoe and your son, my grandson, take priority right now. Never doubt it. But the sooner I get the go-ahead from you, the sooner I can start the transition. I don't think it's wise to rely on Janet's support right now."

"Agreed. She's too volatile. And neither of us are in a strong position." I grunt. "Christ, I'm living a hotel right now."

"You know." My dad's mouth curls into a faint smile. "I can help with that."

"Thanks Dad, but I don't think Zoe wants to live in your basement. Neither do I." Thinking of Zoe's reaction makes me laugh.

"Michael." He groans with exasperation. "Have you never stopped to wonder why your properties sold so quickly at such good prices?"

I give him an incredulous stare.

"Your two Gold Coast condos? Your ownership stake in the Mexican hotel?"

I feel my jaw drop.

"It was me." He smiles with satisfaction. "Agree to come back before the end of first quarter, and I'll return them all to you. Free and clear. Think of it as a signing bonus."

"Wow. That's one hell of a bonus." One thing puzzles me. "Why are you holding onto my mixed use building?"

"Your what?" He answers with a confused look.

"The one that DeadFall MMA leases? It was the first property I put on the market."

"I'm sorry." His head shakes. "That one's gone. I don't have it."

"Fair enough. Thanks for salvaging what you could."

He nods, then grunts as he braces himself against the wall to stand. "I'll let you get back to Zoe." He puts his hand on the doorknob but doesn't open it right away. "Think about it, Mike. Rarely does a man get the chance in life to solve all his problems by taking a single definitive step. Do us all a favor, son. Don't blow it."

"We'll talk soon. And not just about the business."

"I look forward to it." Then he opens the door and exits the stairwell.

ZOE

I STIR AT THE FAMILIAR SENSATION OF SWEET, SALTY LIPS brushing against my sore, parched mouth. Despite the cloudy haze that blocks my path to alertness, Mike's presence elevates my senses.

Impressions of my hospital stay are sketchy but generally positive, given the circumstances. I remember bleeding heavily at Mike's fight, and the wave of panic that had rushed through me. I knew that much blood so late in the pregnancy was dangerous for both me and the baby.

The memories of my son's birth are largely rapid, traumatic, and muddled. The nurses told me my son was alive, that I'd lost a lot of blood and received at least two —three?—transfusions, a life-threatening ordeal that's left me very weak. I felt scared and helpless but determined to live.

Never seeing Mike or our son again was not an option.

Mike caresses my hair, then moves to my cheek with soft downward strokes. I know from his visits this past week he's not trying to wake me. He's greeted me this way since the baby was born. Sometimes he sits for hours, just holding my hand. Other times, he speaks without expecting a response.

Today is different.

I can no longer bear the sadness and worry in his voice. I want to speak to him, comfort him and ask about our son. Today, I have the strength to make it happen.

"Mike. Hon?" I will myself to speak, despite the painful dryness of my throat.

"Hey, Zo-Zo." He plants an excited kiss on my forehead. "Nice to see you awake."

"Any water?" I ask. "So hard to talk."

"They left you some ice chips." Mike takes a paper cup with a plastic spoon from the bedside table.

"Okay," I whisper.

Mike scoops ice from the cup and feeds me with the spoon. It makes feel like a toddler.

"How's the baby?" I ask when my mouth is semi-functional. The nurses told me he was doing okay, but I don't remember when that was. Besides, I want to hear it from him.

"He's fine." Mike's blue eyes overpower me with emotion. "He should be out of NICU by the end of the week."

"You've seen him?" My eyes well with unshed tears. If my body wasn't so dehydrated, I would openly weep.

Mike nods. "Whenever I'm not with you, I'm with him."

"God, I'm so lucky." Relieved sobs erupt from me. "As long as I have the two of you in my life, I can get through whatever comes next. I love you, Mike. So very, very much."

It scares the hell out of me to love someone like him, who's accustomed to swooping in and arranging things the way he wants while making it as easy or difficult as he chooses for everyone involved. But the thought of him not knowing scares me even more.

"I love you, too, Zo-Zo. I have for a very long time." Mike gives me a bittersweet smile. He pauses. "I…wish we'd both admitted it much sooner."

His words alarm me. "But this is a good thing, isn't it?"

"I hope so." He sounds nervous. "We need to discuss to our future."

"What's wrong? Mike, please…" I start to sit up, but he settles me back into bed with a kiss.

"Take it easy, hon."

"Give me the remote. I want to sit up."

He hands me the cord that controls the height of the bed, and I adjust it until I sit up comfortably and look him in the eye. "Please tell me what's going on."

"I made some big decisions this week. In normal circumstances, I would have talked to you first. But things weren't normal, and that's why it needed to get done."

"Go on." I take the paper cup with the ice cubes in it from him, then spoon feed myself a mouthful of ice. Whatever he tells me, I want to be able to speak.

"I'm going back to work for the family business. My

father offered me the CEO position, and I've accepted it." He watches me closely, gauging my reaction.

"Are you serious?" The thought of this warrior sitting at a desk goes against the laws of nature.

Mike puts his hands on his hips and shakes his head. "Trust me to fall hard and fast for the only woman on the planet who'd find being married to the CEO of a multi-billion dollar company a major turnoff."

"Maybe that's why you love me?" I suggest.

"Maybe." He maintains a frustrated tone.

I crunch on a mouthful of ice, trying to find my voice and gather my thoughts. When I'm ready to speak, I blurt out what's on my mind. "Did you do this because I was sick? You don't need to, you know. I'll be fine."

"Don't ask me to parse things like that. I did it for a lot of reasons. Were you a consideration? Abso-fucking-lutely. So was my son. And my parents. What's wrong with that?"

Shit.

This is the answer I dreaded. Will he resent me and our son one day because he felt forced into making this choice for us? No, I can't live with that.

"I know what happens when someone gives up on their goals for somebody else's sake. They end up bitter and resentful. My mother did it. Twice. Once for my own father, who left anyway because that's just who he was. The second time was for Chloe's father.

"He was a kind man who just couldn't keep his shit together. She devoted all her time and energy to keeping him functional and them a couple. But it was too much for both of them. My mother's completely given up on that kind of happiness. It's a soul crusher to want and wish and work so hard but have it end it a failure. I don't want that to happen to either one of us."

"I get why you feel this way. But it's time for you to let this go." He's firm and assertive.

"Let it go? And go along with something we'll both regret? I can't do that, Mike."

Mike exhales a long, slow breath. "Stop pretending you'll walk out of here and get back to life as you know it. You and the baby will need help."

"I know that." I shove another spoonful of ice into my mouth and contemplate his words. What he's saying is true, and during every moment of conscious thought this week I've focused on that reality. It would be a lie to pretend I wasn't counting on help from him.

"You'll be weak for a while, and both of you will need easy access to the hospital for doctor's visits." He rubs my cheek. "We'll stay at my apartment."

"Your apartment? I thought you sold it."

"Long story short, I got it back." He hesitates. "And I don't want to piss you off, but my mom is setting up a nursery there. When you're out and well, you can redecorate it any way you want."

I've consumed enough ice now to shed tears. It's a relief to have a place to live beside my mom's. Mom and I had spoken about Mike living with us while he looked for another place. Mom had agreed but warned me that things would be tight and it wasn't a long-term solution.

This kind of support is alien. It also scares me. What if I become too dependent? "That's a lot of work for her."

"Are you kidding? She's thrilled. And she's asked Audrea for help to make sure it's decorated according to your taste."

"Oh my god." My temples throb. "That's way too much for them."

"You don't have to do everything yourself." Mike sounds annoyed. "The rest of us aren't incompetent morons, you know. We only want to help. And honestly, you need it, so take it easy, Zoe."

"I don't think of you as incompetent. It's just that I, I… can never repay all of this."

"It's not a debt. It's help we all want to give you. And how do you know you won't do the same later? That's how the world works."

I take a deep breath and try my best to let go of my fears. "Thanks, to all of you."

"You're welcome, Zo-Zo." He gives me a relaxed smile followed by a pensive look.

"What is it?"

"You know, Zoe, this week has been total hell. It was touch and go with the both of you, more than once. Going through it at arm's length because we weren't related made it almost unbearable." Mike closes his eyes and shivers. "Thank god Andrea was supportive of visitation. But I never, ever want to go through that again."

Before I can speak, Mike reaches into the hip pocket of his jeans and pulls out a teal box with a white bow. He clutches one of my hands and presents the box with the other.

"What… what are you do… doing?"

"Zoe Inglot, I want you to be the first thing I see in

the morning and the last thing before I close my eyes at night. I never want to see you suffer again, but if you should, I want the right to use whatever resources at my disposal to ease your pain. I want you, Zoe. My biggest regret is not owning it sooner."

I feel my mouth form into a speechless oval. When no words come out, Mike prompts me.

"Hurry up. Open it."

He releases my hand and I pull the ribbon off and flip the spring-loaded box open. Cushioned in white satin is a rose gold band, twisted into Celtic knots around its circumference. Set in its center is the largest, roundest emerald I've ever seen. Not that I've seen a lot, but who doesn't daydream on the internet?

"Emerald is your birthstone. I wanted it to be extra special." His voice is quiet, almost childlike, a stark contrast to the hardened fighter who speaks. "Do you like it?"

"I *love* it." My breathing comes in rapid gasps. "But Mike, it's huge."

"Well, I've already downsized twice to find you a ring that suited your personality without you being preoccupied with cost. It's offbeat and beautiful, just like you. Marry me, Zoe."

"You know I will. It's just…" I struggle for the words.

"What is it?"

"Mike, I'm still in the hospital, and probably will be for another week or two. I haven't seen our son, and we don't have a name picked out. It's no one's fault, the pregnancy was a surprise we've done our best to manage. But I want our wedding to be about *us*."

"Us? Of course, it's about us."

"I mean as a couple. Let's take the time and attempt to celebrate our feelings for each other. Not as parents, or to formalize things for convenience or legal purposes."

Mike's eyes glisten before he nods in agreement. "Take all the time you need. Just don't make me wait forever."

"No chance."

"Come here." He leans down to kiss me.

EPILOGUE

Eighteen months later.

"I really appreciate this, Mr. Garcia."

"It's my pleasure, Zoe. And please call me Rinaldo."

"I'll try. But I feel funny calling one of my teachers by their first name."

"And I feel funny if you don't." He smiles down at me. "You're a grown woman and a mother now. It's time," he warns me when the string quartet starts to play.

He's right. But I can still remember the day back in my sophomore year of high school when Mr. Garc— when Rinaldo introduced me to the pathways program for the university nursing degree. It had been scary at first, but he was patient and held my hand through the entire first year. If it hadn't been for him, I'd be washing dishes somewhere and grateful for the job.

I can't think of anyone else I'd rather walk me down the aisle.

It's a perfect day for a fall wedding. I couldn't have

dreamed of a better location for our ceremony and reception than the rooftop of St. Rafe's. It came together so naturally for us. Mike and I knew we wanted to be married in Chicago and there was no single place more important to us that we could share with our friends than here.

We had come together here. We'd nurtured our fragile, fledgling relationship here. When we needed to hide from the world, we'd sheltered here. Now, we're going to face life and all it holds for us head-on.

"Are you ready?" Rinaldo asks.

"Yes." I've never been more ready for anything in my life.

The heavy fabric of my mermaid gown rustles as I walk down the rooftop aisle. It's full-sleeve, tight along the body with a minimal train. The deceptively simple design is bias-cut from silk moire fabric. Small satin roses adorn the entire dress, each containing a small pearl, added as a gift from Mike's mother.

The dress belonged to Gramms, whose mother had been a seamstress who used her professional network to obtain the fabric for her only daughter's gown. When my mom dug it out of our attic, she'd told me her grandmother originally purchased our small house. This gown makes me feel proud and connected to the women in my family.

My simple metallic headband contains a pattern of colored stones in each oval-shaped ring that frames my face. I couldn't be happier with how everything turned out.

I nod to several guests as I proceed up the aisle.

Friends from the hospital, school and the neighborhood, many more than I thought would attend. Even my mother's brother, Uncle Phil, made the trip.

One look at the front row makes me wish for a camera. My mother sits closest to the aisle, wearing a beautiful silver dress with a blue tulle skirt and a fresh new blunt cut. She whispers instructions into her grandson Gavin's ear as he fusses with his ring bearer's tuxedo while holding the ring pillow with solemn innocence and determination.

Initially, we worried that he would be too young for this. But Mike and I both wanted our son to be part of the wedding. Gavin was eager too, and he gets along well with Doug and is especially close to his Grandma Audrea. We decided to let him walk Grandma 'Audda' down the aisle where the ring bearer's pillow waits for him.

"Am I handsome, Mama?" he asks as I approach.

"Super-duper handsome," I whisper. "Just like your dad."

Gavin smiles ear-to-ear, revealing his front two baby teeth. Eighteen months old. Where has the time gone?

After Gavin was born and my condition had stabilized, the three of us moved into Mike's parents' townhouse while they stayed in their lakeshore home until last Christmas. We had intended to move into his apartment, but then Mike decided that he didn't want to move us out again when renovations started, and after he became CEO of DC-squared.

We'd lived in his parents' townhouse until the Gold Coast apartments were converted into one large unit. At first, I didn't think we'd need all the room, but he wisely insisted and now I'm glad I listened.

"Are you okay?" Rinaldo whispers after I gasp.

"Fine," I tell him, distracted by the sight of Mike standing at the altar, waiting for me.

It's official. My future husband is a damn fine clotheshorse.

His custom, royal blue silk suit looks amazing with the paisley tie and double-breasted vest. He's absolutely killing it with those massive shoulders and lean torso. Mike's shaved his hair out on the sides and left it longer on the top, the way I told him he looked sexiest.

His big blue eyes meet mine, and he gives me a smile with a quick wink.

I flush in response.

Seconds later, I stand at the altar.

Rinaldo helps me up the tiny step, then gives me a kiss on the cheek. "You did good, Zoe." Rinaldo nods at Mike. "He's not too bad either."

"Thanks." Mike shakes Rinaldo's hand before the older man takes his seat.

Mike turns to face me with a serious are-you-okay look. I give him a reassuring nod, and we turn to face the priest together.

The moment possesses a surreal vibe for me. I never thought I'd get married, let alone to such an amazing man in this beautiful, romantic setting. My mother never married, even though there were times in her life I know she wanted to be. *It all worked out for the best*, she'd often say.

But after discovering how transformative being with

the right person is, I honestly hope she finds someone. It's sappy, I know, but when you're as blissfully over-joyed as me, you want everyone you love to experience the same thing.

I glance over at the profile of the man who's the source of blissful joy in my life. Mike's watching the priest, intent on following the cue to deliver his vows. When it comes, our maid of honor, Chloe, takes my bouquet, while our best man, Doug, helps Gavin get into position to deliver the rings.

Mike recites his vows in a clear voice without needing notecards. His eyes never leave mine, making the emotion behind his words inescapable. I do my best to deliver my vows with equal sincerity, joy, and dignity.

"Good job, little man," Mike proudly tells his son, who lifts the pillow with the rings up to him.

"Thank you." I stroke Gavin's cheek and remove Mike's ring.

The next thing I know, there's an amazing kiss, a huge cheer, followed by another amazing kiss.

"Ladies and gentleman," the officiant announces, "I present to you Michael Gavin and Zoe Rosalie Daughtry."

"Hey," Mike greets me as the band announces the First Dance.

"Hey yourself."

"You ready, Mrs. Daughter?"

"I'm not sure. Chloe?"

"Almost done." My ever-helpful sister has pulled me aside because there's a problem with the back of my dress.

Chloe started college a year ago and is crushing it. She jokes about medical school, but I know she's dead serious. I'm so happy to see her thrive.

The band begins the opening chords of "Perfect Symphony." Mike and I had taken a while to agree on a song because there were so many good ones to choose from. But once we heard this one, our search was over.

"Um, Chloe?" Mike asks after the band repeats the opening chords.

"All set," she replies. "Take her away!"

Mike grasps my hand and leads me to the dance floor for the traditional First Dance as a married couple. I put my arms around him and lean my forehead against his chest. It's the first private moment we've had all day.

"Ah," I groan as Mike's hand massages my lower back as we dance. "Thank you."

"How are you holding up?" he asks with mild concern.

"I'm fine. It's the high heels more than anything else." We dance a few moments in silence. "How long do you want to keep this a secret?"

"Until after the honeymoon, at least," he answers. "One unplanned pregnancy in a lifetime is enough. But two in less than two years? That's outrageous, even for us."

"I'm sorry." I'd switched to birth control pills after we'd decided to have more children but wanted to space them out more. "This low-dose estrogen approach is an epic fail."

It's also the reason for an autumn wedding instead of a spring one.

"Well, maybe it's for the best. This last year with you and Gavin, in our own house, has been magical." Mike glances over at our son. All of his grandparents are taking turns feeding him wedding cake. "I love being a father, almost as much as I love you. So maybe having a few kids close together while we're young is a good idea. For us, anyway."

"I think so, too." I look back at the grandparents' table. "Our parents are good people. I'm happy to give our children a chance to know them."

"Thank you, Zoe." Mike chokes up and I look back at him.

"Oh, hey Sweetman? Don't worry. Not now." I caress his lean cheek. "I thought your dad was doing well?"

"He is. The chemo seems to be working. It's just a little overwhelming sometimes."

"Is he is still coming to Mexico with us?"

"They wouldn't miss it. We're taking the jet down on Sunday together." He strokes the back of my neck until I purr. "It was nice of you to suggest that. I know your invitation really moved my parents."

"I don't see why it's such a big deal. It's a great excuse for a family beach party."

"Well, most newlyweds aren't keen to invite their parents and in-laws on their honeymoon."

"And I have little patience with such outdated thinking. It's not like we're newlyweds in the traditional sense."
I raise my eyebrows at him. It makes him grin. "Everyone
has their own room, so we'll have plenty of privacy when
we want it and plenty of company when we don't.
Besides, if Gavin can score a sleepover at the grandparents
occasionally, it'll be a win-win for everyone."

"I like the way you think, Mrs. Daughtry." Mike
gives my rear end a quick squeeze.

"I like the way you agree."

Mike smiles and spins me around so that my back is
facing the band. "Since you brought up the subject of
agreement, there's something I need to speak to you
about."

"What is it?" I smile up at him.

"Remember way back in the day, when I agreed to
not cut you out of decisions for the sake of expediency
or sparing your feelings?"

"Mike…"

"Well, all I've got to say is that it's my wedding,
too."

"What did you do?"

"What I do best. Well, maybe second best." His
wolfish grin appears. "I splurged."

"You splurged?" I repeat.

"Yup." He raises his hand and gestures behind me at
the band.

The music progresses from the opening chords and a
familiar voice starts to sing.

A familiar *live* voice.

I turn to look at the stage where a short, ginger-haired man sings into the microphone. It's *him*.

"You've got to be kidding." I gasp and turn back to face Mike. "He must have cost a fortune."

"Actually, *they* cost a fortune," he replies.

I'm puzzled for a split second until an operatic voice sings in Italian.

"Oh my god." I'm so overcome that I stop dancing and lean my cheek against Mike's chest. We sway to the most incredible voices I've ever heard.

"That's the most beautiful, thoughtful, romantic thing anyone's ever done for me. That's been done for anyone I know." I rasp through tears when they stop singing. "Thank you."

"No, thank *you*, Zoe."

"For what?"

"For being *that* girl."

PLEASE BE MY HERO

Reviews help authors to keep writing books. It's that simple. I would greatly appreciate it if you shared your impressions on Bookbub and your favorite booksellers website. Thank you!

THE HEARTS SO FINE SERIES:

Fighting Hearts

Crazy Hearts

Tender Hearts

THE CASINO PLAYERS SAGA

When an affluent former maid agrees to pay her brothers gambling debts, she gets an offer she can't refuse from a wealthy casino owner.

CASINO PLAYERS TRILOGY BOXED SET, Available now!

Please note, this is a serial and all the episodes are intended to be read in the following order:

Book One, All In

Book Two, Double or Nothing

Book Three, Ante Up

ABOUT THE AUTHOR

Annabeth writes steamy contemporary romances that explore the edges of passion and possibility. Her stories contain characters who exude emotional awareness and authentic human weakness as they journey towards their happily ever afters.

Away from the keyboard, she loves to travel, read and bike, in addition to helping with school activities. She calls creative-friendly Austin, TX home, where her family and menagerie of pets keep her company while she's at the keyboard.

BB bookbub.com/profile/annabeth-saryu

f facebook.com/authorannabethsaryu

a amazon.com/author/annabethsaryu

P pinterest.com/annabethsaryu